RACHEL CLARK'S PRINT COMBO

Nothing on Earth
Their Taydelaan

Rachel Clark

MENAGE AMOUR

Siren Publishing, Inc.
www.SirenPublishing.com

A SIREN PUBLISHING BOOK
IMPRINT: Ménage Amour

RACHEL CLARK'S PRINT COMBO
Nothing on Earth
Their Taydelaan
Copyright © 2011 by Rachel Clark

ISBN-10: 1-61034-637-8
ISBN-13: 978-1-61034-637-5

First Printing: July 2011

Cover design by Jinger Heaston
All cover art and logo copyright © 2011 by Siren Publishing, Inc.

ALL RIGHTS RESERVED: This literary work may not be reproduced or transmitted in any form or by any means, including electronic or photographic reproduction, in whole or in part, without express written permission.

All characters and events in this book are fictitious. Any resemblance to actual persons living or dead is strictly coincidental.

Printed in the U.S.A.

PUBLISHER
Siren Publishing, Inc.
www.SirenPublishing.com

DEDICATIONS

Nothing on Earth

For anyone who has ever looked up at the night sky and wondered.

Their Taydelaan

For Kelli

Siren Publishing *Ménage Amour*

NOTHING ON EARTH

Rachel Clark

NOTHING ON EARTH

RACHEL CLARK
Copyright © 2011

Chapter One

Urgent knocking woke Tara Wilson from her almost-doze. Startled, she moved to the front door and began opening the three locks. At the last moment she gathered enough wits to check through the peephole. This wasn't a dangerous neighborhood, but it was never wise to take reckless chances.

John, her neighbor, stood on the other side of the door, pounding the wood with his clenched fist. She'd never seen him like this. He'd always appeared calm and composed, but at this moment he seemed panicked. As she undid the final lock she wondered why he hadn't called her name. A small, frightened part of her didn't even want to open the door to someone who looked so out of control, even if she did know him.

Was she in danger from this man?

She shook her head sharply. This was John. The man who'd lived next door for almost a year and had never been anything but kind. She took a deep breath, threw open the door, and screamed when a large hand covered her mouth and John pulled her against his solid body.

Hell, he was a big man, and right now, despite her own above average height and self-defense training, she felt very small and very, very helpless.

"They're on the way here. You need to be quiet."

"Who?" she managed to ask with his hand still pressed against her mouth.

"*They* are. I tried to hide you from their scans, but they found you anyway. Please, Tara, just trust me."

Scans?

She tried to pull away from him, but he held her tighter, and panic began to flood through her. "I know you're scared, baby. Please just trust me to protect you."

Baby?

What the hell? They were neighbors, had barely shared polite conversation in the hallway. Why would he think she'd welcome a term of endearment under these circumstances?

This felt too real to be a joke, too frightening to be some sort of prank. John seemed wild, terrified even, and she was fast getting there herself. Adrenaline coursed through her, and she fought his hold, thrashing against the arm that held her around the waist and biting the fingers that kept her silent.

She screamed around the thick digits even as he wrestled her to the floor and pressed his superior weight against her. She'd read stories like this. The nice, quiet guy building a fantasy in his mind and killing the neighbor or workmate or stranger off the street because he thought she should love him. Hell, even if John was suffering from a type of mental breakdown, his actions definitely pointed to her being the one in danger—from him.

Beyond blind panic now, Tara managed to bite him hard enough to make him grunt.

"Baby, please, they'll hear you. Please don't fight me. I need to keep you safe."

She'd heard enough. The most terrifying experience she could ever imagine was happening right now, and it didn't have anything to do with whoever "they" were.

She bit down harder, her desperate screams turning to whimpers of fear as he held her tighter. She felt a tingle at her neck, and then everything faded.

"I'm sorry," he whispered.

* * * *

Tara woke with her head pounding, her mouth dry, and her lips sore and cracked. She opened her eyes to complete blackness, and it took a long time to realize that she was in a very dark room and not suffering blindness. The smallest amount of illumination came from a tiny LED-type light in the wall. She blinked several times, trying to improve her vision but had little success. She breathed heavily as fear invaded her senses and she remembered how she got here.

John.

Tara moved quietly, only then realizing that her hands were bound together and tied to something. Heart pounding painfully, she used her fingers to follow the tether back to its point of origin. She almost cried out loud when she realized that the thick, plastic-feeling rope looped back on itself and was secured between her wrists. She tried to lift the knot to her mouth only to realize that there seemed to be no end. No actual knot or buckle holding the thing together. She tried to stem her rising panic as she used teeth and tongue to try and identify how she was bound. It seemed to be a continuous loop with no beginning or end, and she tugged at the bindings hoping for something to give, for some luck, for divine intervention. None were forthcoming.

She closed her eyes, trying to still her breathing as she listened intently for a noise. Nothing, absolute silence, and it probably explained why she wasn't gagged. If the room was isolated enough or soundproofed enough that she couldn't hear anything, then chances were no one would hear her pleas for help even if she screamed at the top of her lungs.

Swallowing against the trapped feeling and the bile creeping into her throat, Tara tried to get her brain to work rationally. John had taken her, saying that he had to protect her. Protect her from what? Even if he was delusional—and that was looking very likely—chances were that he wouldn't hurt her. Well, not yet at least. She needed to find an approach, figure out what he wanted from her, so that she could maybe talk him down.

He'd always seemed like such a nice guy, and she'd never seen any indication that he was using drugs. Maybe this was a one-off thing. Maybe when the drugs wore off he'd come to his senses and let her go. That was assuming, of course, that he actually remembered where he'd hidden her.

She tried to slow her breathing, but nothing could calm the fear of being left here tied to a wall until she died. She crouched low, bracing her back against the strange metallic wall, as she tried to sort fact from fear.

He hadn't hurt her, and despite the fact that he'd terrified her and drugged her, he hadn't actually damaged her. Nothing hurt, so she was fairly certain he hadn't done anything untoward while she was unconscious.

Everything he'd said indicated that he was trying to protect her. Delusional or not, he believed she was in danger from someone else and that it was his responsibility to protect her. Maybe she could work with that. Go along with his ideas, make him feel like she was cooperating with him until she could get some help. She squashed the fear down and resolved to be a good little prisoner until she could find a way out.

The last thing she expected was a stranger to walk through the door.

* * * *

Alec walked into the room cautiously and switched on the small light in the corner. One thing he did know was that not everyone was as comfortable in the dark as he and John, and he wondered at John's state of mind when he'd left a frightened woman in a pitch-black space. She was already terrified, just judging by the bite marks on John's hand. Despite the fact that they were trying to help Tara, there was no way he was getting close enough for her to sink those teeth into him.

"Are you hungry?" he asked quietly, speaking to her in the same way he'd seen a vet on television speak to an injured animal. She looked at him for a moment, fear, anger, and mistrust crossing her features before she smiled. He didn't trust that smile at all. Animals often bared their teeth before attacking.

"Can you help me?" she asked in a friendly manner.

"We helping you," he said in the same low voice he'd used before. "Are you hungry?"

"Where's John?" She tried to look around him to the open doorway as if she expected the man himself to be standing there.

"Supplies. He back soon."

"Can you help me?" she asked again, this time sounding more desperate. "Can you untie me before John gets back? I need to go home."

"No go home," he said shaking his head. His English language skills were still poor, and he was really regretting not trying harder to learn when he'd had the chance. He searched his brain for the right words. So far she didn't seem to understand his question. "Food. Are you hungry?" He made a motion with his hand that he hoped would translate to eating. She shook her head. He wasn't sure if she was saying she wasn't hungry or that she didn't understand, but she began talking quickly, and he had to concentrate to keep up.

"I need to go home. You have to let me go. John is dangerous. You have to let me go before he gets back."

He thought he understood the words, but their meaning didn't really make much sense. Why would she want to go home? They were coming for her, and he and John had to keep her safe.

He shook his head the way he'd seen John do. "No, they coming. No home. Dangerous."

She shook her head as tears flowed from her eyes. More words tumbled rapidly from her mouth, but this time he missed most of them. She was very agitated, and he wasn't certain why. John had told him she was frightened, and therefore dangerous, so she needed to stay tethered to wall at least until they could ensure her safety.

She kept talking, her words getting louder, and he realized that she would soon be heard by the neighbors if he didn't close the door. Considering her agitated state, and sharp teeth, it was probably not a good idea to lock himself in with her. He turned to leave the room, but she let out such an alarmed sound that he hesitated. Against his better judgment, he closed the door and stayed on this side.

* * * *

Tara tried hard to bring herself back down from hysteria. Even though the situation certainly warranted a panicked response, a small, rational part of her brain demanded that she at least try to think clearly.

She took a deep calming breath, wiped her hands against her eyes as best she could, and then attempted to smile at the stranger.

"What's your name?" she asked, trying to sound friendly.

He pointed to his chest, seemingly confirming the meaning of her question. She nodded carefully.

"Alec," he said in that same deep tone he'd used before. He was a big man. Not quite as huge as John, but just as tall, just as handsome. Too bad they were both delusional.

"Alec, I need you to listen to me," she spoke slowly, trying hard to pronounce the words clearly. She suspected that his English was poor, so the calmer she stayed, the better chance he had of understanding her. "John made a mistake. No one is coming for me."

Alec shook his head. "John protecting you. No mistake."

"No, Alec," she said firmly. "John is wrong. No one is coming for me. I need to go home." Alec titled his head as if considering her words. "Please, you need to help me get out of here."

Feeling more desperate she tried another angle. Tara lifted her arms showing him her bound wrists. "John is holding me prisoner. He is not protecting me. He is abducting me."

"Abducting?" he asked slowly, seeming to roll it around his tongue like he'd never said the word before.

She nodded. "Yes, abducting me. Taking me away against my will."

He nodded as if he understood, but his next words deflated her small hope.

"Yes, not Tara's will, but John protecting." He came closer, approaching her as if he expected her to attack him despite being attached to the wall. Slowly, he reached a large hand toward her face, and she forced herself to stay still as he wiped the wetness from her tears away. "Soon, Tara be safe."

She shook her head as more tears gathered in her eyes. She had no idea who this man was, but it seemed pretty obvious now that he wasn't going to help her.

"Are you hungry?" he asked again.

She didn't answer, just hung her head lower as despair crept through her, stealing her energy, stealing her hope.

Chapter Two

John needed to hurry back to the safe house. Damn, he'd really messed this up. He'd be lucky if Tara wasn't absolutely terrified of him now. He shook his head, trying to oust the misgivings from his mind. He'd done the right thing. Intellectually, he knew that. Tara would've been captured if they'd heard her. He'd had no choice but to ensure her silence. He'd saved her from the unimaginable.

But he doubted she'd ever forgive him.

This had all gone so horribly wrong. He'd wanted nothing more than to let her live her life in peace, on her own terms. He'd watched over her, protecting her from them every single day since he'd found her. He'd tried to keep her life as normal as possible, but now that plan was blown to hell.

How had they known? How had they found her?

He grabbed the last of the supplies, stuffed them into the duffle bags, and piled them into the back of his car. He'd only set up the safe house a few months ago, and other than the soundproofed, hidden room, it was poorly furnished and badly equipped.

Halfheartedly, he threw his tools and some spare parts into the trunk of the car, but he knew he couldn't risk using the equipment he'd used to hide her before. They surely had a way to identify it now. He'd have to design something new, but he had no idea where to start at the moment. He couldn't seem to think past the knowledge that he'd frightened Tara.

He slammed the trunk closed, frustration at his own ineptness not helped at all by the attention-drawing sound. The last thing he needed was the neighbors noticing that he'd packed up Tara's things as well as his and Alec's.

He climbed into the driver's seat, started the engine and, faking a calm he was far from feeling, waved to the elderly woman watching him from her chair on the veranda. By the time he reached the highway, he felt his fear escalating again.

They were closing in.

Tara needed to be saved.

* * * *

Tara's heart leapt into her throat as the door burst open She tugged desperately at the bindings holding her wrists, fear and determination masking the pain.

John yelled at Alec in a language she couldn't identify and then turned his attention to her. She pulled harder against her bonds.

"Stop," he ordered as he came into the room. "Tara, stop. It's just me. It's John."

That did absolutely nothing to make her feel better. John was the man she feared the most. She'd known it was him coming through the door, but he spoke as if she should expect someone else. God, how did she get a starring role in his delusions?

"Tara, stop," he said more quietly. He moved closer, and despite the part of her that wanted to kick him in the balls, she cringed from him like a frightened child. Tears fell from her eyes as she continued to pull against her captured wrists.

John must've realized the closer he got the more terror she felt because he stopped his advance and took a step back.

"Tara, safe," Alec said quietly. She shook her head wildly.

"No, Alec, I'm not safe. John is dangerous. I...I'm not safe."

She saw John's face as she said the words. Oh God, what had she done? She was supposed to go along with the scary man, be a good little hostage, not antagonize a disturbed mind.

"I'm sorry," she sobbed, no longer consciously choosing her words. "I'm sorry. John, I'm sorry. Please forgive me. I didn't mean it." She fell to the floor, her wrists lifting at an uncomfortable angle as the tether pulled tight. She dropped her head forward, her hair falling like a curtain over her vision. She could barely see through the tears anyway, but the hand that touched her head terrified the daylights out of her.

She forced herself to accept the caress without pulling away. She had to go along with his delusions. Her life depended on it.

* * * *

John stepped forward, unable to tolerate seeing her in agony, agony that he'd caused. He wanted to pull her into his arms, hold her tight, and never let her go, but he knew she wouldn't welcome his embrace. Hell, the one and only time he'd held her, he'd sedated her, abducted her, and hidden her in this small room. That wasn't something anyone forgot in a hurry. Oh, and to top things off, he'd tied her to the wall for her own safety.

He knew she was terrified, but he couldn't *not* comfort her. He reached out a trembling hand and touched the top of her head lightly, a little surprised she didn't pull away until he realized she was forcing herself to hold still.

"I'm sorry." He barely managed to force the words past his dry throat, and his heart ached as she continued to sob. "I know I frightened you. I didn't want to, but I had no choice. If they'd found you, they would've taken you, and I can't let that happen."

He caressed the top of her head gently, trying not to frighten her any more than she already was. "Tara, I'm going to take the cuffs off so that you can move around. I need you to promise me that you won't try to run. They'll find you if you leave this room."

She nodded slightly against his hand.

"Tara, baby, I need you to promise you won't run. It's not safe. Not for any of us anymore. You have to trust me to keep you safe."

"I p...promise," she said falteringly as she lifted her hands higher. He saw the reddened skin where she'd chaffed it against her bonds, and he wanted to apologize all over again.

God, he'd fucked this up.

* * * *

She still had her head down when he undid the bonds so she didn't see how he removed them. Inside her head she cursed a blue streak at her stupidity. If he put her in them again, it would've at least been helpful to see how the damn things worked.

Squinting as she tried to see around the dark, little room, Tara tried her best to hide her agitation. John still stood in front of her, and she braced herself not to pull away from his touch. She'd antagonized this man more than enough for one day. She really needed to protect herself and stick to her resolution to be a good little prisoner.

"Tara, Alec is going to stay with you while I work. We have a lot to get through, but I don't want you to be alone."

She nodded again, strangely relieved that she wouldn't be locked in this dark, claustrophobically small room alone.

Chapter Three

Alec watched the way his lover reacted to the woman. He acknowledged a large amount of attraction for the pretty brunette himself, but he could see that John felt far more deeply. Had John fallen for her while Alec had been busily trying to avoid the outside world? Hell, he'd been sulking ever since John had dragged him to this city. He hadn't wanted to leave everything and everyone he'd known just to follow John as he followed his conscience, but Alec had done it because he loved the man.

He could see that John was suffering. Alec understood how much it had hurt John to frighten Tara the way he had, but he also understood the motivation and the necessity.

A sob drew his attention back to Tara. She sat with her head dropped forward, her hair covering her pretty face as John undid the tether. He didn't need to understand the words his lover murmured to know what he'd said, but the last part caught him by surprise. John left the room, closing the door firmly behind him, before Alec could utter a protest.

It wasn't that he didn't want to try to comfort Tara. It was just that he knew how much John needed his reassurance right now. The look on John's face when Tara had begged for Alec's help would likely haunt him for a very long time.

She couldn't have hurt him more if she'd had a weapon. The soul-destroying words had hit John very hard, despite the fact that they'd both expected them. Alec carefully moved toward where Tara sat on the floor rubbing her reddened wrists. She looked up as he got closer, and he again cursed his reluctance to learn English. All those times he'd refused to practice the language with John now seemed petty and spiteful and, quite frankly, childish. He hadn't gotten his way, so he'd sulked and made John miserable, and now here they were, trying to protect a terrified woman who had absolutely no understanding of the danger she was in.

And he, dumbass, selfish bastard that he was, held no ability to explain it to her.

"Tara, I sorry," he said as he moved closer still. She kept her head down, and he could still hear her crying, so he wasn't even sure she'd heard him. "Tara, I sorry," he said again and reached a hand toward her. Even the threat of those straight, white teeth didn't worry him at the moment. The man he loved needed him to comfort this woman while he worked to keep them all safe. He would do this no matter what.

She looked up at him, eyed his hand, then glanced back up to his face. "I sorry," he said again, and this time she nodded in response.

"I know," she said quietly. "Everybody is sorry, even me, but I don't think it's going to save us."

He shook his head, a little annoyed at her lack of faith in John. John would protect them both, he knew that for certain, but then he realized what she meant. She thought John was the danger. He needed to make her understand, but his lousy language skills held him back. Hell, he could make this situation worse just by using the wrong word in the wrong context at the wrong time. He whispered a promise to John that he would learn English as fast as he could.

"What language is that?" she asked quietly.

"Not English," he answered with a small smile. Hell, he didn't even know what his language was called. He'd just always spoken it, and everyone around him had done the same. He didn't even have enough skills in English to explain that he didn't even know.

She frowned at his answer, but another sob escaped instead of words. Slowly, he moved to settle his arms around her. She held herself away from him, so he just sat still on the floor, waiting for her to move closer to him. He took a small amount of comfort that she hadn't pulled away, but he'd watched her withstand John's touch even though he terrified her, so he didn't exactly congratulate himself on his tactic.

She shivered in his arms but eventually leaned against him and let him embrace her. Alec had no idea what to say. Even in his own language, he wasn't sure what would be appropriate here, so he simply held her close, and eventually she began to relax against him.

It felt so different to be the one offering comfort. He'd grown so used to John taking care of him that he'd forgotten that he wasn't the only one who needed support. He closed his eyes as memories of his selfishness of the past year surfaced. He'd really hurt John. John still loved him, despite the fact that he'd acted like a selfish brat. He really was a lucky man, and he needed to find a way to make it up to his lover and best friend.

Several hours later, Tara had finally fallen asleep. He'd carried her over the small cot in the corner and sat on the floor beside the bed holding her hand. She whimpered in her dreams, and he smoothed a large hand over her head. She really was a beautiful woman.

The door opened quietly, and he glanced up to see John standing at the doorway, his body language telegraphing his tense worry.

"Asleep?" John asked in their language.

"Yes," he answered in English, determined to let his lover know he had his support and that he would learn as quickly as he could from now on. Alec carefully placed Tara's hand back on the bed, moving slowly, silently, so that he wouldn't wake her. He stood and walked to his lover.

He didn't say a word, just wrapped his arms around John's waist and held on tight. John exhaled heavily as he pulled Alec closer, and Alec felt even more wretched for having made his partner feel so alone. They were in this together, and Alec vowed silently that he would do everything he could to help his lover.

"I love you, baby," John said very quietly against Alec's ear. Alec lifted his face and pressed his lips against John's warm mouth, showing him without words just how much he loved his man. They kissed each other until the passion became too intense for where they were. John pulled away, panting hard as he whispered in Alec's ear, "I need you."

Alec nodded, wanting desperately to please his love. They'd been a couple for years, and it had been Alec's own fault that they'd grown apart. Here was his chance to close that distance and begin to heal their fractured relationship.

John led him into the main room, pulled the metal door closed, and then engaged the lock so that Tara was safe. He lifted Alec off his feet as he kissed him harder, more deeply, more urgently. John's hands shook as he worked at the buttons of Alec's shirt, and Alec helped by ripping it over his head impatiently. He also quickly undid his pants, dropping them to the floor so that his engorged cock sprang free. Almost immediately, John's warm hand wrapped around Alec's swollen shaft and began tugging on him.

John's grip was hard, almost painful, but Alec welcomed the sensation, welcomed the chance for his lover to take him the way he used to. Alec didn't even know there was a table behind him until John lifted him onto it and tilted him backward. The thick, blunt finger was almost a shock as it penetrated him without lubrication.

"Baby, I need to be inside you, but I can't remember where I put the lube."

"It's okay," Alec whispered, knowing this was going to hurt. But John did what he always did, protected Alec from any and all pain, and instead wrapped his hand around both of their cocks, rubbing them together as he pumped quickly. The intense, rapid sensation had Alec's balls pulling tight, his breathing erratic as his lover rushed him to an intense climax. Hot cum hit his naked chest as John kissed him wildly. The kiss went on and on until Alec thought he might faint from lack of oxygen.

Finally, John lifted his head and whispered, "I love you."

Alec fell back onto the table, unable to hold himself upright, but grunted as he bumped his head against something hard.

"Perfect." John laughed quietly as he grabbed the bottle of olive oil from behind Alec's head. As he'd always done, John took care to prepare him properly. By the time John fit his fat cock to Alec's opening Alec was so ready he was half out of his mind with need.

John pushed the head of his cock inside. He held still a moment, and then it was as if his control finally snapped. John pushed hard, filling Alec's ass, stretching the muscles deliciously. Alec gasped as John set a fast pace. He lifted Alec's legs up and outward, holding him apart as he plowed into him over and over. Already Alec could feel his own cock returning to life, and he cried out when John grabbed him by the balls and said one word—"Come."

Pearly-white streams coated Alec's stomach. John stilled in his ass, the pulsing beat of his cock comforting Alec as John found his own release. John gasped for breath and held his lover tight. It hadn't been like this in a long time, and he mourned the loss as John pulled out of his ass.

"Go have a shower, baby," he said as he helped Alec off the table. "I need to check a few things, so it would probably be a good idea if you slept beside Tara tonight."

"What about you?" Alec asked worriedly. He'd slept next to John every night for the last six years, but tonight it seemed far more important—for both of them.

"I don't think my presence would help Tara rest, but I'll try to get a few hours out here. Hold her tonight. I think she needs to know she's not alone."

Eager to help anyway he could but reluctant to leave his lover alone, Alec wracked his brain for a workable compromise. Before he could come up with anything that made sense, John was lifting him onto his feet.

"Shower," he whispered as he turned Alec toward the bathroom door.

Unable to think and unwilling to disappoint, he followed John's instructions.

* * * *

Tara woke as a clean, soap-smelling arm slid around her middle. She lay facing the wall, but even without being able to see him, she knew it was Alec climbing onto the bed beside her. It felt strange that she could accept his comfort so calmly despite the circumstances. Even the fact that Alec seemed to be John's lover didn't really matter right now. The comfort of being physically close to another human being meant more at this moment than any other time in her life.

"Why are you doing this?" she asked quietly. She didn't want to antagonize Alec, but she really needed to understand how he fit into all of this. Did he just follow his lover blindly, not knowing the details or the circumstances he may be dragged into?

"Tara, safe," he replied softly.

Tara rolled over to face him in the dim light. Searching his face for something she couldn't quite define, she tried again. "Safe from what? What is it? Who is it that John thinks he's protecting me from?"

Alec shook his head, but she didn't have a clue if it was because he didn't know or because he didn't understand her words.

"I want to go home," she said brokenly, not really caring if he understood or not.

"Home not safe. Sleep," he said as he rolled onto his back and gently guided her head to his shoulder. "Sleep, John fix, be better. Safe."

She sighed tiredly but let him maneuver her into a comfortable position for both of them, very relieved to realize that Alec was fully dressed. Whatever was going on here, it didn't seem to be a kinky sex thing. Well, not yet at least.

Chapter Four

He held her soft curves against him, a little surprised at how different it felt to lie beside a woman. It had been many years since he'd held a female close, and he'd forgotten just how different the experience could be compared to sleeping next to John. John was huge, all muscle and very loving, and most often slept with his arms wrapped around Alec, holding him close, even when they'd been arguing. Sleeping next to John made him feel safe and protected and loved. But sleeping next to Tara bought forth a whole lot of different emotions. For the first time in a long time, he felt responsible for another person and didn't want to let John down again by failing to comfort Tara.

He could feel the tension in her body, the way she held herself rigid even as she tried to feign being relaxed. He lifted a callused hand to her face and swept a loose curl away from her eyes. She truly was a magnificent specimen. She was quite tall for a woman, but she was built in beautiful proportions, neither fat nor skinny but rather a lovely example of curvy perfection.

Alec pulled her just a little closer, amazed at how much he enjoyed the gentle press of her breasts against his side. Even fully clothed, he could feel the swell of her womanly flesh.

She'd asked him a question, and he hadn't quite caught the words, but he felt fairly certain he knew what she'd asked. Basically, why? She wanted to know why this was happening to her, and he had absolutely no way of explaining it. He hated that it was necessary for both Tara and John to go through this, but he couldn't see any way around it. John said they were coming, and Alec trusted him. John had never been wrong before, so Alec saw no reason to doubt him now.

* * * *

John woke suddenly as his torso tilted forward. He hadn't even realized he felt that tired, so the small loss of consciousness was a little unnerving. He tipped his head from side to side trying to loosen the muscles in his neck and shoulders. He'd been working on this for so long that even his eyelids were numb.

He ran a hand down his face, glared at the device in front of him, and then pushed his chair away from the table and stood up. His spine felt stiff and sore, so he moved around the room, stretching and flexing his arms as he went over the design again in his head.

He suspected that it was the actual absence of a signal in the area that had alerted them to Tara's existence. They'd found her simply by not finding her. A blind spot in their scans, though not unheard of in itself, had most likely led them to her. He'd always known he ran that risk, but he hadn't expected them to find her quite so quickly.

He'd been working on a portable device that would mask her signal from the scans, but now it seemed he needed to disguise her, not just hide her. She needed to show up on their scans, but she needed to somehow give a false reading.

He cracked his knuckles as he shook his head in frustration. He needed to create both a scan dampening field and a signal generator, and even though he had an idea how he might do that, he didn't have the tools or materials necessary to make it. He wasn't even sure he'd be able to *get* the parts he needed.

But he couldn't sit here all night. He had to at least try to find what he needed. He glanced at the clock. It was almost four in the morning. If he left now he'd maybe make it back here before lunch. He looked at the wall where the hidden door stood. She was safe in that room, for now at least, but he needed to make sure that she couldn't escape and give away her whereabouts.

He needed to make sure that Tara and Alec had enough supplies so if he took longer than he expected, they would at least be comfortable. He moved quickly, gathering items and food from the kitchen. The hidden space also contained a small bathroom, so he grabbed toiletries and other necessities as well.

It took several trips, but he managed to grab everything he expected the two of them to need for two or three days. He had no intention of staying away so long, but he knew from recent experience that things didn't always go as planned.

He removed the small panel that hid the lock override, punched in the sequence to open the door, and then quietly dragged the supplies into the room. He stilled at the sight before him. Even though he'd told Alec to hold Tara, he hadn't quite prepared himself for what the sight might do to him.

A curious jealously wormed its way through him at the same time that his cock swelled with excitement. The man he loved with all his heart and the woman he'd loved from afar were entwined, fully clothed, on the small bed. She slept with her head against Alec's shoulder, her arm over his chest and her knee bent slightly to fit over his thigh. She looked tired and drawn, but also vulnerable and desirable and very beautiful.

Alec looked even more handsome at that moment than John could ever remember, and he wanted nothing more than to climb onto the bed and pull them both into his arms.

But just remembering the fear in her voice was enough to place a damper over what he wanted. He'd scared her—badly—and he had no idea how to fix it. At least she'd accepted Alec's presence. At least she wasn't living through this terrible situation alone.

He bit back the sigh that wanted to escape as he leaned over and shook Alec gently. "Baby," he whispered close to the man's ear. "Baby, I need to go out for supplies."

Alec roused quickly, seeming to wake from only a very light sleep. "Why?" Alec whispered in a sleep-roughened voice.

"I need to track down some parts, but I'll be back as quickly as I can." Alec nodded his understanding, his hand moving up his body to rest over Tara's hand that lay fisted over his heart. "You'll be safe in this room, but it's extremely important that Tara not leave. They'll come as soon as they detect her signal, so she has to stay in this room."

Alec nodded his understanding but stiffened when Tara moved against him.

"What language is that?" she asked quietly.

"Tara," John said softly in English, "I didn't mean to wake you. Everything's okay. Just go back to sleep."

"No," she answered stubbornly. "I asked you a reasonable question, and I expect an answer. What language is that?"

He smiled slightly at her attitude. She was locked in a small room with two men who outweighed her five times over—men she probably believed to be delusional—but she still found the courage to stand up to him. Maybe that's why he'd given up everything he and Alec had ever known to try and protect her.

"There is no name for it. This is the language our people speak. Everyone speaks the same language, so it has never been given a name."

"Your people? What country are you from?" She looked to be getting angry now, and John, though relieved to see her natural, normal personality, worried that she would soon remember the fear she'd felt yesterday. She'd stopped short of actually calling him crazy, but it had been obvious in her behavior that she thought it.

"We don't have a country."

She opened her mouth to say something, but Alec moved slightly and pulled her tighter against him.

"Tara, trust John, please." The words were awkwardly pronounced, but he was grateful to Alec for his effort. Learning the local language had been a cause for argument for so long in their relationship that John had given up hope of Alec ever being able to communicate with Tara. Hopefully, Alec knew enough of the language to keep her calm while he was gone.

Speaking in his own language again, he gave quick instructions to Alec, told him he would lock the door from the outside, and all the while tried really hard to avoid the angry look on Tara's face. Guaranteed, he wasn't going to be very popular once he locked them both in again.

Chapter Five

Alec watched John watching Tara. He'd always known his lover felt deeply for the woman but somehow had convinced himself that despite all of their relationship issues, he was secure in John's love. Now he wasn't so sure.

When John looked at Tara, his face lit with a type of pleasure that Alec hadn't seen in a very long time. Not since they'd first met and their relationship had been shiny and new and full of possibilities. He pulled Tara closer even as he realized the strangeness of his thoughts. He wasn't just jealous of John's feelings for Tara but also the possibility that Tara might have feelings for John that excluded him. He knew it was ludicrous. Tara was terrified of John, but still, what happened when she learned the truth? Would she still push John away?

When she asked about their language, Alec had been willing to tell her almost anything. Anything at all to put her mind to rest. Hell, he'd make up a name for his language if that's what it took to help her relax.

John finished telling him everything else as quickly as possible. He smiled, and Alec thought he would lean forward and kiss him good-bye, but he stopped himself midmovement and started to pull away.

Alec couldn't stand the thought that his lover would hide their relationship in front of a woman who was quickly becoming very important to them both, so before he could talk himself out of it or think rationally, he reached over and gripped the back of John's neck.

Before he could react, Alec pulled John toward him. Slightly off balance, John placed his hand on the bed, leaning over Alec as he smiled sadly.

"I love you," Alec said clearly, cursing himself for not knowing how to say it in English. He wanted Tara to know how he felt about this man, but he supposed the fact that he was about to kiss his lover good-bye might help break the language barrier.

John looked relieved and hopeful and a dozen other emotions before he exhaled heavily and crushed his lips against Alec's relieved smile. Alec tried not to analyze why John had thought he wouldn't want to kiss him in front of Tara, so he deepened the kiss even further.

He felt Tara move beside him and had a moment of terror when he realized she may be about to use their distraction to her advantage and make a run for it. He almost laughed aloud as both he and John moved to hold her still without actually breaking their kiss. Tara wriggled a moment more before giving up and lying limply in their hold.

Finally, John lifted his head, and Alec wanted to cry at the relief he saw there. He'd hurt his lover so badly over the last year, he hadn't even noticed when John had begun to doubt his love. Oh hell, he really needed John to know that he loved him and supported him in every way.

"Keep Tara safe," John said as he leaned forward for another quick kiss. "I'll return as quickly as possible."

Alec nodded, determined to live up to his lover's faith in him. He felt Tara tense as John left the room and locked the door behind him.

"It be okay. Trust John," he said to Tara as he smoothed the hair away from her eyes. She nodded, and he hoped that she at least was feeling less in danger and more protected than she had yesterday.

"You love him, don't you?" she asked. He looked at her quizzically, hearing the words but not really understanding them. "You love John," she said again as she nodded her head.

"Love?" he asked carefully. Was that the word he needed?

"Yes, love as in care for John. Live with John. Love him with all your heart." She pressed her hand to Alec's chest and then to his lips. "You love John."

"Yes," he agreed, hoping he understood her correctly. "Alec love John. Trust John. Tara trust John."

* * * *

Strange as it sounded, Tara was beginning to trust Alec, despite the fact that he obviously loved and trusted John. Alec seemed to genuinely care about both of them, and that could be the difference between life and death.

When John had first entered the room, she'd been terrified. She knew that she was very literally cuddled up to John's lover, and she'd braced herself for the fit of jealously that would surely follow.

But instead, John had stood over them both. She'd barely had the courage to open her eyes the small fraction necessary to see him, but fear had won over cowardice. If attack was imminent, she wanted to at least see it coming. John had watched them both for a long moment, and if she'd had to guess, she would say that he was not unhappy to see them together. In fact, he appeared quite pleased that she and Alec seemed close.

It had taken every cell in her body to stay still while they talked in their own language, but eventually her need to know had overridden her sanity, and she'd demanded details.

The smile John had given her had been a little unnerving, and she couldn't decide if he respected her for standing up to him or thought she was simply a lunatic for taking on two men who were so much larger and far more dangerous than herself. She still couldn't believe she'd lain there and watched them kiss for almost three seconds before it occurred to her that this was her chance to escape. John had left the door unlocked, and in their distracted states, she might've had a chance to run.

Strange how exciting it had been when they'd both reached for her and held her immobile as they continued to kiss. It had been one of the more intimate moments of her life, which had made the experience even weirder. Maybe she'd been locked in this windowless room for far longer than she realized. She certainly seemed to be suffering from some sort of mental incapacity.

"Sleep," Alec urged as he pressed her head back onto his shoulder and played with the curls of her hair. Part of her wanted nothing more than to lose herself to unconsciousness, but the rest of her demanded action.

"I need the bathroom," she told Alec, wondering how on Earth she was going to explain her need to a man who didn't understand the language. An unnerving image of a game of charades entered her mind, and she spoke louder, very aware that yelling a language the man didn't understand was not going to make him understand any better, but she couldn't seem to stop herself.

"Bathroom! I need the bathroom. If I don't get to pee in the next five minutes we are going to have a very messy problem on our hands. Bathroom," she shouted in annoyance. "Dammit! How the hell did I get kidnapped by someone who doesn't even understand the fucking language?"

She glared at him angrily, frustration that he couldn't understand her shouted words making her irrational. "I want a fucking bathroom. I want a fucking toilet, and I really want a fucking shower!"

"Shower?" he repeated, raising his eyebrows as if he understood that particular word. "Tara, shower, yes." He nodded as he said the stilted words.

"Yes, Tara wants a shower," she said tiredly, no longer caring if he understood or not. She shook her head. Nature was going to be appeased one way or another. Dammit.

"Shower," Alec said as he levered off the bed and held his hand out for her. After a moment of uncertainty, she placed her hand in his and let him help her to her feet. He dragged her behind him as he moved to the corner where the small light hung suspended from the ceiling.

She watched in uncomfortable fascination as he ran his hands over the wall. It seemed more and more likely that he'd misunderstood her words, and she found herself wondering about his sanity as well. Just as she was about to surrender to despair, Alec grunted something, and with a small click, a door popped open in the wall.

"Shower," he said grinning at her. There was no light beyond the open doorway, and she was very reluctant to step into such complete blackness. "Shower," he said again and nodded at her to enter.

She shook her head, the terror of waking to pitch-black darkness last night returning to choke her. "No," she said as she shook her head more vigorously. "No, it's dark, and I can't see, and I'm scared, and I want to go home and—"

She didn't get to finish the frantic words as Alec pulled her into his embrace. She hadn't realized she was crying until Alec's oversized knuckle swept the moisture across her cheek. He held her close, mumbling words she couldn't understand, and she clung to him as she shook.

Chapter Six

God, how could he be so thoughtless? The woman was already scared witless and here he was trying to shove her into a dark, little room. He murmured words of comfort, knowing that she wouldn't understand him, but hoping she would recognize the tone.

She clung to him, her whole body shivering in reaction. Damn, the harder he and John tried, the worse they seemed to make the situation for her. Alec held her until she sagged against him, her energy gone. He had no clue what the words "I'm sorry" were in English, so he just held her and silently cursed his own inability.

When she seemed calmer, he held her and twisted so that he could reach the light just inside the doorway while showing her with his actions that he was not going to push her into the room. He fumbled against the smooth wall, his fingers sliding against the cool tiles until he found the switch.

The immediate brightness stung his eyes, and he closed them for a moment, but he felt her lift her head away from his chest.

"Bathroom," she said quietly.

He looked into the tiny room. Bathroom? The room that held a shower was called a bathroom? He filed this away for later reference at the same time realizing that Tara could help him learn more of the language. Chances were they were going to be locked in this room for quite a while, even if John got back quickly. Teaching Alec the local language just might help Tara set aside her fear for a while.

Tara stepped back, wiped her eyes with her fingertips, and gave him a small smile. "Bathroom," she said as she stepped into the small space. "Shower," she said pointing at the shower stall.

He knew the word shower. There wasn't an actual translation for the word in his language, so both he and John had used the local word for the cleansing area.

Tara saw the toilet in the far corner and headed over to that spot. Her hands moved to the clasp of her jeans, but her hands stilled, and she gave him a pointed look. He wasn't quite sure what she wanted, but when she tilted her head towards the door, he figured she was probably asking for some privacy. He could give her that. He turned his back and stepped through the doorway. He pulled the door closed part way, uncertain if she would welcome the claustrophobic feeling of being locked into an even smaller space than the room where the bed was.

A few moments later she opened the door and asked him something about the shower. She lifted her shirt between thumb and forefinger seeming to indicate something.

"My clothes. Clothes," she said. He lifted his own shirt in the same manner, and she nodded. "Clothes."

When he finally realized what she was asking for he felt like a bit of an idiot. She wanted a shower and clean clothes. Putting on clean clothes was what one did after a shower. He must be losing it to miss such a simple meaning.

He nodded and turned back toward the bags John had dragged into the room earlier. "Clothes," he said with a smile.

Tara fell to her knees and opened the overstuffed bag.

* * * *

Tara opened the bag quickly.

"Clothes," Alec said again, but they weren't just anybody's clothes, they were her clothes. Hell, one of them—probably John—had gone through her wardrobe and filled a bag with practically everything she owned. She gasped when her hand found silk.

Someone had even cleared out her lingerie draw. God she hoped that wasn't some sort of warning of things to come.

"Tara, shower, be little."

She looked up at him a frown contorting her face as she tried to understand his meaning. "Little?" she asked.

He opened his mouth, but no words came out, and she could see the frustration marring his handsome features. It was obvious he wanted to say much more, but he simply didn't have the knowledge of her language.

"Little shower?" she asked again, trying to reassure him as well as understand him. "Do you mean a short shower? Get in, get out, very quick shower?" He still looked at her with that frustration brewing in his eyes. In desperation she moved to pantomime, pretending to turn on the taps, wash her hair and body, and then turn off the taps. "Little shower," she said hopefully.

He nodded like he wanted to agree but wasn't quite sure he should. She glanced at her watch, surprised to see that it wasn't yet five o'clock. She was assuming, of course, that it was morning, although, with the absence of natural light, she really couldn't be sure about anything.

Her watch. She lifted it to Alec's face, pointing to the second hand as it did its rapid sweep around the dial. "Little shower," she said, making a circle in the air. He nodded, seeming to understand what she meant.

"Little shower," he said with a smile as he made three full circles in the air with his finger. Three minutes.

"Got it," she said smiling. "Three minute, little shower." She was so happy that they finally seemed to understand each other that she didn't really care why she had to have a quick shower. Locked in this little room, the one thing they did seem to have in abundance was time.

Unwilling to think any harder on anything other than her upcoming three-minute shower, Tara rummaged through the bag, no longer surprised to find her own towels, deodorant, and toiletries on the bottom. John seemed to be a very thorough man. Unfortunately, considering her current circumstances, that probably wasn't a good thing.

No. No thinking. Shower.

She moved into the small tiled room, careful to close the door over but not actually shut it. She quickly stripped off her clothes, uncertain whether her three minutes began when she entered the room or stepped into the shower but unwilling to waste a moment. The water was hot almost instantly, and she tilted her head forward so that the water ran over neck and shoulders.

She hadn't realized just how cramped the muscles were until she tried to loosen them a little, and she titled her head side to side in an effort to release the knots. She lathered shampoo into her hair, massaging her scalp quickly wishing she had more time. She hurried through her shower, hopefully rinsing away the stench of fear of the last twenty-four hours.

"Tara," Alec said quietly from the other side of the door.

"Yes, finished," she said as she turned off the running water. She wrapped the towel around her but realized with dismay that Alec had taken her clothes out of the bathroom. Securing the end of the towel she peeked around the door, hoping to be able to ask why he'd done that.

Alec was hovering at the doorway, seeming quite anxious. When he saw her he reached for her wrist and dragged her into the main room. He closed the door firmly and turned to her with an apologetic look.

"Not safe," he said as he pointed at the door.

She had no idea what he meant. The bathroom wasn't safe? Granted, bathrooms had their dangers, but she got a feeling that he meant more than the usual household accidents.

He gestured to her clothes sitting neatly on the bed and then turned his back and politely waited for her to get dressed. That, she didn't need to be told twice.

* * * *

Alec turned his back hoping that she understood his meaning. What he really wanted to do frightened him almost as much as it would frighten her. He'd barely spent time with any female in the last ten years—actually no time in the last six living with John—but he found himself thinking of all the possibilities and comfort a man could find in a woman's body.

It was a ludicrous idea on several counts. She was confused and frightened, and even if she did seem receptive to his ideas, he'd never know if she gave herself to him in genuine affection or if she was just trying to appease her crazy abductors. If he was a betting man, he'd certainly pick the latter.

Besides, it was a rather moot point. He loved John, had committed his life to him a long time ago, and there was no way he would ever betray the man's trust. John needed him now more than ever. There was no way he would hurt him like that.

Alec could hear Tara dressing quickly and thanked whatever deity may be watching over him. Now, if they could just find something to do for the next however many hours it took for John to return.

"Alec," she said quietly.

He turned slowly just in case she wasn't quite finished, relief pouring through him as he noticed the loose-fitting shirt and baggy jeans. He'd seen some of the clothes in her bag and by choosing these she sent a rather clear signal—she wasn't dressing to impress, so, despite his unruly hormones, they were thinking the same way.

"Are you hungry?" he asked, using the only phrase he was completely sure of its meaning.

She nodded, and he moved toward the small mountain of food that John had dragged in here with everything else. She walked over to stand beside him, and he felt very grateful that at least she wasn't frightened of him like she was of John.

His heart constricted just thinking of his lover. John had spent the last year watching over this woman, protecting her without her knowledge, probably learning everything about her. Alec knew John's feelings for Tara were strong and extremely complex, but he also knew that John loved him and would never do anything to hurt him or Tara, even if that meant denying his own happiness.

Alec wished a million times over that he hadn't been so difficult to live with this past year. John had deserved so much more from him, but Alec had behaved like a spoiled brat denied his favorite toy. If he'd just bothered to learn the language, things would've been so much easier right now.

Alec and Tara both grabbed some food and headed back to the bed, the only place to sit other than the floor. They sat in silence as they ate, Tara seemingly lost in her own thoughts. After several moments of fairly comfortable silence, a thought occurred to John, and he turned to Tara quickly.

"Tara, Alec, English," he said stiltedly.

She looked at him like he was a puzzle to figure out. He searched for the word he wanted, but frustration crept through him as he realized he didn't even know the word, so he had no way of remembering it. How many times had John asked him to *learn* English? Learn? It probably wasn't the word he needed, but maybe Tara could decipher his meaning. He tried again.

"Tara learn Alec English."

"Alec learn English? Tara teach Alec?" she said with a number of hand movements, touching her mouth and pointing between the two of them.

"Teach," he said slowly, nodding his head, and hoping that was the word he needed. She smiled softly and leaned over to grab his hand. She pointed to his hand, touching all the fingers and his palm.

"Hand," she said watching him intently. He dutifully repeated the word, flexing the appendage as he said it. She nodded and pointed to his fingers one at a time. "Finger, finger, finger, finger, thumb."

He smiled at the musical lilt to her voice as she taught him her language. Hopefully they could both get something out of this—English language skills for him and a distraction from the reality of their current situation for her.

* * * *

John drove as fast as he dared. It had seemed to take forever to track down what he needed, but he'd finally gathered the raw materials and tools he would need to build a portable dampening field. He still hadn't figured a way to create a false signal, so he was hoping that if he kept the field small—only big enough to surround Tara—that it would attract less attention from their scans. A little blind spot was far more common than a big blind spot, and if Tara restricted her movements to a small area, she should be safe until he could create the false signal.

He rubbed his eyes tiredly. He still had a lot of work to do, and he couldn't afford to lose concentration. As much as he disliked the taste of coffee, he actually looked forward to its effects, and as soon as he got back to the house, he planned to brew a big pot.

Lost in his thoughts, he almost didn't notice the markings and registration plates of the car in front of him. Adrenaline and fear coursed through him when he realized the familiar vehicle was heading to the safe house.

One eye on the road, John checked his pistol. He had no wish to kill anyone, but there was no way in hell he would let them take Tara.

Chapter Seven

Tara giggled at Alec's attempt to pronounce "abdomen." She supposed it was a rather peculiar word, and his comical attempt probably explained why children were taught belly and tummy rather than the medical terms.

She shook her head and smiled as he tried again. "No, how about *belly*," she said, patting her middle. They'd managed to work their way through most of the nouns in the room, but Tara had no idea how to teach John other words. She'd never learned a second language herself, so she really had no clue what to teach him next.

Deep in thought, she yelped in surprise when the door flew open. Two police officers leveled their guns at Alec as they called her name. "Tara Wilson?" one of them inquired. Relief washed through her, but Alec pushed her behind him and stood to confront the two men.

He started to speak rapidly in his own language, and she tried to move around him, tried to reassure him that it would be okay. These were the good guys, but maybe Alec's loyalty to John made it difficult for him to understand that.

She tried to explain to him, but he cut her off. "No, Tara. Not safe."

"Yes, I am," she shouted loudly. She wriggled against his grip, but he held her tightly behind him. Desperate to be rescued, Tara wriggled against his hold, calling for the police officers' assistance. Alec seemed like a great guy, but if he was going to support John in this terrifying situation, she sure as hell wanted away from him, too.

"Release her," one of the officers yelled.

Terrified that they were going to shoot Alec, Tara called out, "He doesn't speak English."

Alec continued to yell in his own language, and Tara cringed in fright. The situation was getting crazier by the moment, and she truly feared the only possible end would be when someone got shot.

She kicked and screamed and made it near impossible for Alec to hold on to her. He squeezed her hands harder, pulling her arms around him so that she essentially hugged him around the waist.

"Tara, not safe." He grunted as she kicked him harder.

"Let me go," she screamed, her voice getting louder, her tone more hysterical.

The sound of a single bullet was deafening in the small room, and Tara screamed as she felt part of Alec's massive weight fall onto her. She twisted, finally managing to pull her arms free. He fell to his knees and grabbed for her ankle as she flew past, adrenaline making her movements exaggerated and bouncy.

One of the officers grabbed her, and she clung to him gratefully as Alec called to her in his own language. He yelled at her, his words rapid, his tone desperate, pleading. The officer who held her laughed at the same time that his partner replied to Alec in what seemed to be his own language.

Tara screamed as the gun fired twice more, and Alec fell to the ground, his blood staining the carpet in this small room. Tara struggled out of the officer's hold, terror pulsing through her at their actions. Alec had no longer been a threat, but they'd executed him. Blindly, she ran, laughter loud behind her.

She made it to the front door, but her hair was grabbed in a cruel fist, and she fell backwards, barely managing to get her hands underneath her so that she didn't land flat on her back. The police officers face hovered in her dimming vision as he spewed malevolent words that sounded like Alec's language.

The man laughed sadistically as he grabbed the front of her shirt and ripped the material with a single pull. She screamed, thrashing frantically as his fingers hooked into the front of her bra.

But his fingers went lax, and he fell forward his large body pressing painfully against her for a moment before he moved sideways. She barely had time to register the third person in the room before he moved passed her toward the doorway to the hidden room. She wanted to call his name, she wanted to throw her arms around him, and she wanted to apologize in every language known to man for not trusting him.

John pointed a strange device and activated it just as the second man dressed like a police officer came through the doorway. The man's smile faltered as he saw John, but his body crumpled a moment later.

John merely stepped over the man's prone form and entered the room where Alec lay dying, if he wasn't already dead.

"Tara," John called urgently, "I need your help. Get in here!"

Tara glanced at the front door as self-preservation warred with human decency. Alec had tried to protect her, and he'd been shot for his trouble. Like it or not, she was the reason the man lay dying. She hurried into the small room that only minutes ago had been her terrifying prison.

John had moved Alec onto his back and currently held his hands pressed against the wounds in Alec's chest. "Tara, grab the green duffle bag in the corner."

She moved immediately to do as he ordered. "Where's the phone? I'll call an ambulance," she said as she placed the bag beside him and moved close to Alec's head. Alec's neck was at an awkward angle, but she knew little about medicine, so even though she wanted to make him more comfortable, she had no idea if she should. Held helpless by her lack of knowledge, she stood by as John zipped open the bag and pulled out more strange gadgets.

"They used human weapons," he said to her urgently. "I have to get the bullets out before I can close the wounds."

He broke open a small package and dragged on latex gloves. He unwrapped another item, a tool that looked like a strange version of needle-nose pliers, and then pressed his finger deep into one of the wounds and slid the pliers in beside it. Alec grunted from the pain, and Tara hoped that was a good sign.

"Sorry, baby," John said quickly. "This'll just take a moment."

True to his word, John pulled the pliers out and dropped a misshaped piece of metal onto the ground. He repeated the action for a second bullet, but as he checked the third wound, Tara's thought processes finally cleared enough for speech.

"It went straight through," she said urgently.

"Are you sure?"

She nodded. "I was behind him."

* * * *

John had already figured out by the blood spatter covering Tara's face and hair that she'd been quite close when Alec had been shot, and even though it was a relief to know that she hadn't been injured, his blood ran cold at just how close he'd gone to losing them both.

He grabbed the small medical unit he'd been able to smuggle off the ship and started to seal the wounds in Alec's shoulder, chest, and abdomen. The instrument would knit the flesh back together with a mixture of technology and accelerated healing, but he would need to put in a drain so that any blood that had poured into the abdominal cavity would be removed before it caused a problem. It would also give him a chance to monitor if the bowel had been punctured. He sure didn't need that complication, but he had to take precautions. At least being shot by a bullet didn't introduce the same contaminants as a knife wound could, so infection seemed unlikely.

Alec's eyes fluttered but didn't open as John pushed the drain into place and sealed the flesh around it. "John," he said through blood-spattered lips.

"Yes, baby. You're going to be fine. Just rest while I get things organized. We need to leave here before they send more agents. Tara, go have a quick shower. Dump the clothes. We don't have time to wash them, and I don't want to be on the road with a bagful of bloodstained garments."

She nodded her head, wide-eyed as his meaning apparently sank in. She glanced down at her arms, finally noticing the blood covering her upper body, and for a moment he thought she might give in to hysteria.

"Baby," he said to her in a soft yet commanding voice, "don't look in the mirror. Just strip off, get into the shower, and wash everything. Okay?"

She nodded her understanding, seeming to shake herself into action, but she moved stiffly, awkwardly. For a moment he worried that she'd been injured by the man who'd attacked her in the foyer, but she moved quickly to do as he asked.

"John," Alec whispered, his voice sounding raw and weak.

"It's okay, baby. As soon as Tara is finished, you and I are going to have a hot shower together."

Alec smiled just a little. "Figures," he said. "We finally get a chance to shower together, and I'm too tired to take advantage of you."

John released the breath he hadn't even realized he'd been holding. It would be a few weeks before Alec fully recovered from his injuries, but at least now John had a reasonable belief that his lover would be okay. He'd been very worried that Alec had lost too much blood, but at the moment it seemed he would recover without needing a transfusion. John really hoped that didn't change.

Tara came out of the bathroom, a large towel wrapped around her, and headed straight to her bag. She rummaged for clothes as John lifted Alec into his arms and carried him into the bathroom. Carefully, he sat the injured man on the side of the tub and held him upright as he pulled Alec's blood-soaked clothes away from his skin. Awkwardly, John pushed Alec's jeans down his legs, but after several moments of frustration, he ripped the material and pulled the tattered denim away.

Finally, he had Alec stripped, and he carefully lowered him onto the floor of the shower stall and then stepped back to tear off his own clothes. He angled the water away from Alec as he adjusted the temperature and then stepped in to quickly wash himself down. He then lathered shampoo into Alec's hair as a brief pang of loss caught him unawares. When was the last time he and Alec had been this close? Not just physically but in an emotional sense. They spent most of the last year either fighting or ignoring each other. Hell, he hadn't taken very good care of his lover in months, and he resolved to do much better in the future. He'd almost lost Alec today, and he was going to make sure that he didn't waste another moment of their time together.

John lifted Alec onto his feet and held him tightly as the water rinsed the shampoo from his hair and the blood off his back. A soft sigh escaped Alec's lips, and John couldn't help but press a kiss to his lover's forehead.

"Can I help with anything?" Tara asked through the slightly open door. He was relieved to hear her voice. A small part of him had expected her to take off while he was distracted. He'd be able to locate her fairly quickly, but it was far more convenient not to have to.

"We're almost done," he said as he twisted off the taps. "Would you mind dressing Alec while I hold him steady?"

He was probably asking a lot here, but even though she was traumatized and terrified, he still needed help to get Alec into his clothes without hurting him. Having Tara's assistance would make it much easier.

"Sure," she said cautiously as she stepped into the bathroom. "I'll try. Just tell me what to do."

He lifted Alec into his arms. "We might need to do this in the main room," he said as he looked around the cramped tiled space. Tara nodded her agreement, grabbed the towels off the vanity, and led the way into the other room.

Once in the main area, John lowered Alec's feet to the ground and held him close as they both dripped water onto the carpet. Tara stepped forward, stood on her tiptoes to rub the towel gently over Alec's hair and then lower down his back, over his buttocks and thighs, and then knelt to dry his lower legs and feet.

"Okay, Alec. Time to turn around," she said in what he guessed was her imitation of a nurse's tone. Carefully, he turned Alec in his arms and tried to hold his dry parts away from his own still-dripping abdomen.

Tara briskly dried the front of Alec, hesitating over the spots where the bullets had hit. The device had worked quite well, and now only a pale patch of skin covered each entry wound.

"How?" she asked as her startled gaze collided with John's.

Chapter Eight

"We have a lot to explain to you, Tara. I'm just sorry that we couldn't shield you from it," John said quietly.

She nodded, not really understanding anything that he said. Well, not really understanding anything that had happened in the last twenty-four hours but very willing to hear an explanation now that her life had been almost literally turned upside down.

"Clothes?" she asked, determined to get Alec to safety before she started demanding answers.

"Leather suitcase over by the sleeping man at the doorway," he said, indicating it with his chin. She moved toward the bag but hesitated as his words hit her.

"Sleeping?" She couldn't quite hide the fear in her voice. Strange how she felt quite comfortable when she thought her and Alec's attackers were dead. Knowing they were only asleep worried the hell out of her. She'd never seen a dead body, never wanted anyone to be dead, but right this moment she would have preferred it over the thought that the sleeping man might wake up.

Shit, this was one majorly fucked-up day.

"Yes, baby. They're only sleeping. I'd rather not kill anyone, no matter how much they might deserve it." She could hear the anger in John's voice but also the quiet determination to hold true to his own values. Hell, she owed him a major apology.

She moved toward the suitcase, very grateful that she was able to drag it away from the unconscious man without him twitching. John's soft voice called her attention again just as she was thinking of kicking the man who laughed as he tried to kill Alec.

"Baby, he'll be out for hours, but we need to be on the road long before then." His words were said in a low, soothing voice, and she wondered if maybe he could read her mind or at least her intent. Shit, she wouldn't be surprised. After the things she'd seen today, anything seemed possible.

She grabbed track-pants, a shirt, and underwear from Alec's case and hurriedly pulled them onto him. It wasn't until he was fully dressed that the thought he and John had both been completely naked finally occurred to her. John still was.

"I'm going to lower him to the floor near this wall. Can you just make sure he doesn't slide sideways while I pull on some clothes?"

She nodded quickly and placed herself beside Alec's exhausted form. She wriggled so that his arm was slung over her shoulder and some of his weight rested on her. Alec mumbled some words, and she looked over to John for a translation. John stared at his lover with an amused expression on his face.

"What did he say," she asked softly, wanting to know what could put a smile on John's face at a time like this.

"He said that he finally has a beautiful woman in his arms, and he's too tired to do anything about it." Tara blushed all the way to the roots of her hair. She could feel the heat travel up her face even as she watched John smile at her reaction as he dressed.

"I'm sorry," she blurted, worrying that John might be offended by his lover's semiconscious flirting.

"Don't be," he said seriously. "You are a beautiful woman with a kind heart, and any man would be lucky to hold you."

That blush sure wasn't going away. She hugged Alec closer as John repacked the bags with everything not covered in blood and hauled them out to the car. On his final trip he gathered Alec in his arms, and she followed them both into the vehicle.

"Where are we going?" she asked. She didn't really care where they went but rather that they avoid encounters with police who didn't really seem to be police.

"We need to head into the mountains," he said as he arranged Alec in the back seat. "There is a cave system about two hours from here that should shield you from their scans. Hopefully, I can build the technology we need before they find you again."

She nodded even though she had absolutely no idea what he'd just said. Well, except for the part about caves. She wasn't keen on caves—had always been frightened of the dark—but she'd survived in that black little room even when she'd been terrified. She'd withstand anything if it meant they'd be safe.

* * * *

Just over two hours later, John drove the car straight into the cave mouth. He didn't want to leave the vehicle anywhere where it might attract attention. This was thick bush land with few visitors, but a seemingly abandoned car might just attract attention from the authorities and end up alerting the people he hoped most to avoid.

Tara looked at him, worry stamped all over her face. He wondered if she was afraid of the dark, a thought she confirmed a moment later when she asked if he had a torch.

"It's going to be okay, Tara. Alec and I both have very good vision even in pitch black. We'll keep you safe." She nodded, her expression one of absolute faith in him. For a brief moment he allowed himself to feel the relief that gave him. Things had gone so badly yesterday that he'd worried she'd never trust him. At least now he had a chance to explain. "Stay here while I make sure no animals have taken up residence since I was here last."

She nodded and glanced over her shoulder at Alec sleeping comfortably on the back seat. John moved to open the car door, but she leaned over and grabbed his arm.

"John," she said, seeming to search for words. "I...I'm sorry. I'm sorry I didn't trust you. I'm sorry Alec got shot. I'm sorry you almost lost him because of me." The wobble in her voice suggested she was very close to tears, and he wanted nothing more than to crush her to him and hold her until she realized this wasn't her fault. Instead, he leaned forward and touched the soft skin of her cheek with his callused hand.

"This isn't your fault, Tara. I knew how dangerous it would be to try and hide you from them, but I also know that neither Alec nor I could stand by and let it happen."

She nodded her understanding as a single tear rolled from her eye. He smoothed it away with his thumb and leaned forward to press a gentle kiss to her mouth. "Tara, I will never regret making the decision to protect you. Never."

"Me neither," a rough voice said from the back seat. It was only then that John realized he'd spoken his native tongue. Tara gave him a small smile as he repeated the words in English and translated Alec's words as well. "We will protect you, sweet Tara, never doubt that."

He left the car before she could say anything else.

Chapter Nine

Three weeks later, John was no closer to getting the portable generator working than he had been back at the safe house. Every time he tried to miniaturize the technology, it created a fatal flaw and the dampening field failed to work. He wanted to throw something in frustration, but he didn't want to frighten Tara.

She and Alec had spent the last three weeks working on his English, and John had watched the bond between the two of them grow. At first she'd insisted on John and Alec sleeping together, obviously aware of their relationship, but Alec had convinced her to sleep in his arms as well. Every night, the three of them curled up on the camping mattress and fell asleep.

He ached every moment now. To be so close to both of them but to just hold them was simply keeping him hard throughout the day and night. He'd often laughed at the description "blue balls," but he was fast wondering if he was about to see the phenomenon firsthand.

"Earth to John," Tara said as she handed him a cup full of steaming black coffee. He took the foul liquid gratefully, hoping that the caffeine boost might help solve his technological dilemma.

"Thanks," he said and turned back to his work. It took him a moment to realize that she hovered beside his elbow still. He turned to look at her, and she blushed that pretty shade of pink that he was definitely coming to think of as his favorite color.

"I was thinking that maybe you're concentrating too hard. Maybe you need to take a step back, relax for a while, and work off some steam. I could give you and Alec some privacy."

His cock sure liked the idea considering the fact that it was about to undo the damn zipper all by itself. Holy hell that hurt.

"I'll just go read by the fire," she said as she tried to move away. He stood and caught her wrist before she could step away. He saw Alec's nod of approval as he said the words he'd wanted to say for months.

"Please stay." He leaned forward and pressed a soft kiss to her mouth, and she gasped as Alec stepped up behind her and wrapped his arms around her middle.

"We want you with us," Alec whispered into her ear. She shivered as his hands lifted higher and grazed the underside of her breasts. "Please say yes," he said in the deep low voice that never failed to turn John on. She watched John, staring into his eyes as she said the word guaranteed to light up his insides.

"Yes."

* * * *

Tara groaned as Alec's hands moved even higher and flicked over her distended nipples. She'd been in an almost constant state of arousal since that first night when Alec had insisted that she sleep in his arms. Knowing that John slept behind him was enough to have her slick with want.

She knew the two men were in a committed relationship, and there was no way she would ever mess with that, but being invited into bed by two of the sexiest and most amazing men she'd ever met was simply too much temptation to turn down.

John kissed her softly, running his tongue over her lips before pushing past and exploring inside her mouth. She moaned as Alec undid the snap to her jeans and pushed them and her underwear to her ankles. John broke the kiss only long enough to allow Alec to lift her shirt and bra over her head, and then he returned to devour her senses.

The cool air caressed her skin as she felt Alec's hand slide down over her tummy and the fingers tangle in the dark curls that hid her clit. His fingers toyed with her rapidly swelling flesh for a moment longer before dipping lower and thrusting into her throbbing pussy. A second finger joined the first, and she rose up on her toes as his thumb found her clit and ran across the bud over and over.

Her legs shook as John's hands found her nipples and plucked at the sensitive peaks. She tried to widen her stance, but with the jeans still twisted around her ankles, she fell forward into John's strong arms. He held her, pulling her further off balance so that she was bent almost in half, her ass pointing at Alec.

"I always knew this was a beautiful ass," Alec said as his hand continued to drive her to the edge. His other hand smoothed over the soft flesh, squeezing slightly before he leaned over to kiss each cheek. John laughed quietly as she reached over and lifted his shirt so that she could suck and lick his nipples. He stopped laughing, though, when she dropped her hands to his waist and pushed his jeans to his knees. His cock sprang forward, and she wrapped her fist around him before he could even think about stopping her.

She was not going to be the only one coming with her pants still around her ankles. She lowered her mouth to his cock and licked the mushroom-shaped head with one long, wet swipe of her tongue. He wobbled at the knees as she lowered her mouth and sucked him inside.

"Oh, Tara," Alec said from behind her as his fingers doubled their effort. "I need to be inside you. Please tell me it's okay."

She nodded against John's cock, but blunt fingers tangled in her hair and lifted her head away. Even the fingers in her pussy stopped moving.

"Say the words, baby," John said in a raspy voice, "or this stops right now."

She tried to see his face, but he held her hair and refused to let her look up. "Yes," she said, giving him what he wanted. "Yes, I want you both to make love to me, and to each other. Please. I need you both."

She heard Alec lower the zipper on his jeans, and then the blunt head of his cock pushed into her slick flesh. She gasped, and John chose that moment to push his solid length back into her mouth.

They both began to move, holding her between them, supporting her awkward position as they pounded into her in unison. She'd never given head quite like this before, and as John fucked her face, she wondered why such rough treatment felt so damn good. Alec shuttled in and out of her pussy, his hold on her hips controlling her movement, her feet barely touching the ground.

She screamed around John's cock as Alec's clever fingers found her clit and squeezed. Her whole body shook as they both slammed into her, her orgasm spreading slivers of heat through every part of her body and soul. She swallowed fast as she felt John's orgasm begin, the hot strings of pearly cum coating the back of her throat as she tried to keep up. Alec stilled inside her, and she could feel his excitement climbing as she sucked the cum from his lover's cock.

As she finally let go of John's thick shaft, Alec lifted her and inched over to the workbench behind John. Careful not to dislodge his hard cock, Alec arranged her, facedown, over the edge of the desk. John placed his hands on her shoulders, effectively pinning her down as Alec started to rock into her throbbing pussy again. His fingers found her clit and circled around and around the oversensitive flesh as she panted against the table surface.

John leaned over her, his mouth close to her ear. "Have you ever had a man in your ass?" he asked, the words a low, sexy throb.

"N...No," she managed to stutter out as a thick digit played with the pucker of her anus, pressing harder and harder against the sensitive ring of muscle. "One day soon Alec is going to fuck your hot pussy while I take your ass. Both of us will fill you, stretch you and make you feel like there's only the three of us in the whole universe."

She panted harder as his dark words wound their way through her mind, and Alec's thick finger pressed past her tight ring of muscle and breached her ass. Orgasm spun closer, her whole body tightening as her pussy and clit swelled with excitement.

"I think she likes that idea," Alec said as he pushed his finger deeper into her ass.

"I think so, too," John said next to her ear. "But this time, I'm going to fuck his ass while he fucks that sweet pussy. Would you like that, baby? You'll feel every time I thrust into his ass echoed in your pussy. I'll be fucking you both."

She swallowed, her vision blurring as her brain went into overload. John moved away, and she turned her head to watch him slick his cock with lube and then moved behind Alec. She felt the first touch. Alec's cock pulsed and leapt inside her pussy several times before he surged into her harder and groaned. She felt every thrust, knowing the rhythm came from John as he fucked his lover.

The combined torment twisted her insides, rushing her to orgasm. She screamed as the fingers on her clit squeezed at the same time that the finger pressed all the way into her ass twisted slightly. Heat roared through her veins, her body shaking against the rough wood as Alec's cock pulsed hot cum deep into her core.

No longer able to move, barely able to breathe, she lay on the bench like a limp dishrag. Alec managed to pull his cock out of her before John moved him slightly and pressed his face against the table next to hers. She watched the bliss on his expression as his lover fucked him. She leaned over to kiss him softly just as John roared his release and fell forward onto Alec's back.

They lay there panting for a while, and then John opened his eyes and smiled straight into her heart. "Hello, beautiful," he said quietly.

* * * *

John lay pressed over the top of his lover as their woman smiled into his eyes. And she was their woman. No way would they ever let her go now. He'd never experienced anything so incredible in his life, and at this point, wasn't even sure his knees were going to work well enough for him to extricate his softening cock from Alec's ass.

"I love you," Alec said quietly, and for a moment, John wasn't sure who he was talking to. Tara's confused expression answered the question, and her eyes darted to his, her expression one of guilt and sorrow. John shifted awkwardly so that he could look her directly in the eyes.

"Baby, I want him to love you, just like I love you."

He wasn't quite sure what to make of the fact that her eyes nearly rolled into the back of her head when he said it. He quickly found the energy to move, careful not to hurt Alec as he pulled away.

He gathered Tara in his arms and pulled her close. Alec ducked under his arms and wrapped his arms around them both.

"Tara, it's okay if you don't feel the same way. We just wanted you to know how we feel."

"But you both love me," she said sounding bewildered. "How can you both love me? And what about your relationship? I don't want to damage the relationship you two have."

"John and I will always love each other," Alec said confidently. "And now that we both love you, as well, that just makes it better." He let go of John's waist so that he could lift Tara's chin and place a soft kiss on her mouth. "Take a chance, sweet Tara. This is already something special. Why not let it grow? I know you can love us both. You just need to give it a try."

She burst into tears, and for a moment panic wrapped around John's heart and squeezed tight. He crushed both of them to him even tighter.

"Tara?" Alec asked softly.

"I think I love you both already," she said shakily, "but I'll never forgive myself if it damages your relationship with each other."

"Never," Alec said, smiling. He reached up and kissed John and then lowered his head to Tara's mouth. "Now, that that's sorted, first I need to untangle my feet and then I need a bath," he said on a chuckle.

Tara wobbled when she went to move her feet, and only then did John realize the source of Alec's humor. All three of them still had their pants tangled around their feet.

"Okay," she laughed happily. "Next time we all get naked first."

Chapter Ten

Alec laughed as he lifted Tara into his arms and carried her to the bathing area. They'd set up a simple camping shower that, thanks to a few tweaks from John, worked remarkably well. She managed to kick off her clothes as they moved, so by the time he put her on her feet, she was stunningly, beautifully, completely naked.

His cock rose with interest even as his mind raced with thoughts. Tara had taken the explanation of who they were and why they were here very calmly, maybe a little too calmly. It was an awful lot for a human to understand, and a part of him wondered if she'd gone into some sort of denial. After all, it's not every day that two aliens abduct a woman to save her from being abducted by aliens.

"What are you smiling about?" she asked happily as he stepped under the water with her.

"Hmm, I'm smiling because I finally have you where I want you and now I can have my wicked way."

She laughed as he'd hoped she would. He didn't really want to think about the possibility that she may believe she was having a bizarre dream or nervous breakdown rather than being hidden in a cave for the last three weeks with a couple of guys not of this planet.

"I think you already had your wicked way, but I'm sure I can find something interesting for us to do."

She slid down his body, her hands smoothing down his water-slick flesh until she found the part of him most eager for her attention. She swiped her warm tongue over the rapidly swelling head as he groaned and locked his knees. Damn, he really needed to be inside her.

"Not so fast," John said as he stepped under the water flow and pulled Tara into his arms. She went willingly, the smile on her face reassuring Alec that she was very, very happy. "I want to watch him eat your lovely pussy."

She blushed the most amazing shade of pink, and Alec grinned when he realized it traveled the length of her body, not just her face and neck.

Alec stood just out of the water spray and watched John use the soap to cleanse and arouse the woman in his arms. Tara shrieked as he pulled away, her movements jittery as she tried to find relief from his torment, but he wouldn't allow her to come. Alec's cock grew harder each moment John teased her to the edge of orgasm and then held her still while she whimpered with need.

"Come here," he said to Alec, who quickly obeyed. Tara twisted in his grip, trying to latch on to Alec, trying to force him into letting her come, but John quickly immobilized her. "Kiss me," he ordered.

Alec stepped forward, willing to give John anything, to do anything he said, trusting him to deliver the most intense sensations like he'd always done. Alec lifted on his toes and kissed his lover with all the passion he was feeling at this moment, careful to not crush the woman between them. She whimpered as she kissed his chest, nuzzling her face against the smooth flesh of his pectoral muscles.

John broke the kiss. Seeming to drag in a deep, shaky breath, he twisted to turn off the spray. Tara took advantage of his momentary distraction to slither out of his hold and into Alec's, rubbing herself playfully against him. She laughed happily when John grabbed her from behind, threw her over his shoulder caveman style, and dropped a firm smack on her backside.

"I have plans for you," he said as he held his hand out for Alec to grasp. He walked them over to the sleeping area and then knelt to put Tara down on the low mattress. He placed his massive hand over her abdomen. "Now, are you going to behave, or will I have to put you over my knee?"

Her eyes darkened with desire even as they widened in surprise. John caressed the skin under his hand as he laughed softly. Alec tried to hide his own surprise. The sweet woman they'd been guarding for so long had turned into a sultry temptress whom neither of them could deny. Hell, he'd spank her all she wanted if it meant she'd stay with them always.

"Not now, sweets, but we will definitely explore that kinky side. Soon," John promised. "Lift your knees," he said as he helped to arrange her in the position he wanted. When he was satisfied with her pose he turned to Alec and smiled. "Come here, baby. I want to watch you tongue our lady to an explosive orgasm." He turned his attention back to Tara. "And then I am going to fuck this pretty pussy until neither of us can walk straight."

Tara visibly shivered at John's words, and Alec felt his cock harden even more. He climbed onto the mattress, positioning himself on his knees as he lowered his face and inhaled her sweet fragrance.

John pushed her legs even wider as Alec placed his tongue over her slit and licked along the swollen flesh. She bucked against him, but John moved to hold her down as Alec pushed his tongue deep into her slippery pussy. She moaned, her legs quivering as he held her swollen lips open with his fingers and tormented the engorged bud of her clit.

Alec felt her juices flowing freely and rolling down to her ass, and he took the opportunity to up the stakes. She screamed as he pushed his thumb deep into her ass at the same time that he bit down gently on her clit.

Her entire body shook as her release hit her. John let her go as she writhed in ecstasy, and Alec moved out of the way as John lifted her and drove that massive cock in with one deep thrust. She clawed at him as her orgasm climbed higher, and he pounded into her harder.

Alec moved closer, happy to watch the faces of both his lovers as they fucked each other into ecstasy. John grabbed him by the neck and kissed him possessively as he rode Tara's orgasm and reached his own.

* * * *

Tara watched her lovers kiss passionately as she gasped for breath. Every muscle quivered and pulsed with exhaustion as she physically recovered from yet another momentous orgasm. She wasn't exactly a virgin, but she'd never quite experienced anything like sex with these two amazing men…aliens. Oh hell, did she have to remember that part right this moment?

"What was that thought?" Alec asked.

Over the last three weeks, she'd admired his ability to learn, and both he and John had proven a certain attention to detail, but she could've done without the part where they saw every little expression she made. She shrugged her shoulders, trying to avoid the awkward topic.

"Tara," John's stern voice admonished.

She knew that tone and had learned very early on in this little adventure that John wouldn't let up until she gave him a full explanation. He could practically smell half-truths, and she'd never been a convincing liar anyway, so her only way out of the situation was to tell him the truth.

"I was just wondering if I should worry about…uhm…the pitter-patter of little alien feet." She tried to smile, tried to make it a joke, but the worry was just a little too real.

Both men stretched out on the bed on either side of her. John grabbed her chin in a firm hold and made certain he had her full attention. "We would never put you at risk that way," he said gently. "Several days of treatment with a synthesized hormone are required before a human woman can conceive our child. We wouldn't do anything like that without consulting you first."

She sure hoped her expression didn't give away everything going on in her head. "Uhm…okay. That's good to know." She closed her eyes, hoping that was the end of the conversation, but they popped open again when his full explanation hit her. "Wait. You mean it's possible?"

"It's actually why they want you," Alec said quietly as he gathered her into his embrace. Her eyes flew to John's, and he confirmed Alec's words with a nod.

"W…What happens to the women they take?"

Tara could see the silent communication going on between the two men and wasn't shocked at all when Alec pulled her closer and suggested she get some sleep. She struggled out of his embrace and hauled herself into a sitting position.

"What happens?" she ground out through clenched teeth. The coward in her didn't want to know, wanted to live in blissful ignorance, but the woman needed an explanation. Needed to understand how she fit into this crazy new world she'd suddenly found herself in.

"They're used for breeding," John said quietly. "They are fed hormones that keep them in a constant state of arousal and then assigned to several males until successfully impregnated."

"Assigned?" she asked, trying not to throw up. John nodded sadly, and she tilted her head as she tried to understand his mood. He seemed to carry a lot of guilt on this topic, and she really wanted to know why. This wasn't just disgust at his people's behavior but something deeper, something closer to home.

Only one question came to her mind. "Why?"

"It's a long story, Tara, but we won't let them take you, so you don't need to worry about it." He ran an agitated hand through his hair and then rolled off the mattress. "I have to go into town to pick up more supplies. Do you need anything?"

She shook her head. John had already thought of everything, including the women's supplies she'd need in less than a week, assuming, of course, that her cycle wasn't affected by recent unusual events.

She could feel his anguish but had no idea how to comfort him, and he certainly made it clear that he didn't want it. He pulled his clothes on, his movements smooth and coordinated like always, but with a swiftness that suggested a need to leave quickly. Tara twisted to look at Alec's face, but he just kissed her forehead and urged her to sleep.

She lay in his warm arms and listened to John get in the car and drive away. Her heart thumped harder as panic crept through her. She needed to comfort him, hated the way she'd made him feel that first day, and now she really wished that she hadn't asked the question. Unfortunately, her need to know outweighed all of that.

"Alec?"

"Are you sure you want to know?" he asked softly. She nodded her head against his chest and rolled over to face him. "Okay, but first you need to know that as soon as John learned the truth he did everything he could to put a stop to it, and when that failed, he gave up almost everything he had in the world to try and protect you and others like you."

She nodded again as her eyes misted with tears. She already knew John was an honorable man. She wouldn't have trusted him otherwise.

"Several generations ago the birth rate on our planet started to decline. Medical advancements gave our people a longer life span and more choices over lifestyle, including when they had children and what sex the babies were. Many couples chose to have only one or two children and slowly, over a few generations, it became apparent that there weren't enough females being born. Governments and scientists tried to reverse the trend, but it pretty much continued. These days, females make up less than one percent of the population."

She couldn't quite imagine a population made up of almost all men, but she could certainly understand the implications. Without enough females, every generation would produce less offspring and eventually the race would die out.

"So that's why they abduct human females? So they can breed and produce the next generation?"

"That pretty much sums it up. The problem for John, and for me, is not what they're doing but how they're doing it. Few human women are compatible, so basically they track down the ones that are, abduct them, and force them to breed." He swallowed heavily like he was trying to keep down the contents of his stomach. She could relate. Her lunch was threatening to make a reappearance, too.

"The general public has no idea that human women are sentient beings. By the time they are seen, the breeding council has pumped them full of hormones, and all the men find are lesser beings desperate to mate. The drugs reduce them to mindless sex slaves, unable to talk, unable to think clearly, unable to defend themselves. The scientists even brag about how they manipulate the babies' DNA so that the children are intelligent. Nobody knows that human women are already intelligent."

"So how did you and John find out that it wasn't the truth?"

Alec looked really uncomfortable now, and she almost told him not to answer. Almost.

"John was a collector. He studied for years to join their ranks. He was so proud when he graduated. I can still see the expression on his face." Alec smiled just a little, seemingly lost in the memories of easier times. "He couldn't wait for his first collection assignment, but it turned out to be the experience that changed his entire life."

"What was his first assignment?"

"You." Alec smiled softly.

"Me?" she asked in a squeaky voice.

He nodded and pulled her back into his arms. "You were his first assignment. Even after his superiors explained the real situation to him and his teammates, John had been willing to do his duty simply because it's a necessary thing to keep our planet alive. Once he realized that human women were as intelligent, if not more intelligent, than the men on our planet, he started to see things differently. He couldn't stand by while human women were being used in such a way. On that first assignment, he managed to hide you from the scans, make it back to the planet, collect me, and move us both here."

Alec looked more uncomfortable with every word he said.

"That must've been hard for you," she said, trying to stay rational. A really big part of her wanted to rage and throw things, but she also realized it wouldn't help the situation at all.

"It was, but I made it even harder for John. I spent months sulking and refusing to believe what he told me, even when I lived next door to you."

"You lived next door? With John? I never saw you. How is that possible? We were neighbors for almost a year."

He looked really sad now, like he carried a ton of regrets. "I refused to leave the room. Refused to learn the language. I hurt him so much, and I didn't once stop to wonder how hard it was for him. Well, not until they came for you." He shook his head, lost in the memories. "I've never seen John scared. I didn't even know he could get scared."

She lifted a hand to smooth across the wrinkles marring his forehead. "He loves you deeply," she said quietly.

He nodded his acknowledgement and continued talking. "I've got a lot to make up for, but I love him, and now we both love you, so we can build a future together. Well, as soon as we can figure a way to hide you permanently."

She knew John had been trying to build some sort of device that would hide her from their scans, but she'd watched him grow more and more frustrated over the last few weeks. The materials he needed just didn't exist on this planet, and every alternative had failed.

"John has also spent quite a bit of time trying to build a version of the scanner the ships use to identify women like you, so that he can find them first and hide them like he's hidden you."

"If he hides them all, won't your people die out?"

He nodded sadly. "It's a possibility, but what is happening now is unacceptable. Maybe if John can hide enough women, he can force the breeding council to reveal the truth."

"If people knew the truth, would it change things?" She couldn't help but wonder if, when the future of their species was the cost, whether Alec's people would choose to ignore such cruelty.

"I don't know," he said as he rubbed his hand down his face. "There are probably more like John, but I don't know how we would find them. I know John tried to change things, and judging by the comments made by the guy who shot me, I'm guessing it put his life and mine in danger. Hell, he didn't even tell me. Just did everything he could to protect me and let me treat him like crap while he did it. I owe him a lot."

"So do I," Tara said quietly. Yes, she owed John more than she could possibly repay. How could she thank someone who saved her from a life of slavery and abuse?

* * * *

John drove carefully, making sure he stayed under the speed limit despite his desire to gun the engine in anger. He knew what Alec and Tara would be talking about. Tara was one stubborn woman, and he knew from the months watching over her that when she wanted an answer, she always found a way to get one. He had no doubt that right at this very moment Alec would be telling her everything.

His gut ached. He'd left for just one reason. He simply couldn't relive those days.

He could still see the terror in the eyes of the women who'd been captured on that collection trip. He'd heard the anguish in their voices, seen the tears in their eyes, watched helplessly as they'd been drugged and tested and reduced to nothing more than mindless sex slaves. His heart had broken when he'd seen proud, intelligent human women stripped of their most basic rights.

It had been the hardest time of his life. His squad leaders had assigned him to guard duty as punishment for failing to collect a specimen, and his fellow collectors had joked and teased him for his failure. The whole time he'd held his tongue. He'd kept his temper, held back the urge to rescue the women, and had tried to figure out who to approach when they got home.

Surely their leaders didn't understand that human women were intelligent. Surely this was happening without their consent. Surely someone somewhere had a conscience and enough power to put an end to this barbaric practice.

But he'd been wrong.

Maybe he should've gone public, should've contacted the news outlets and released the scandal that way, but he'd held to the belief that he lived among decent, rational beings, and it had cost him dearly.

He gripped the steering wheel tighter. He'd accepted every abusive word from Alec as his due. He'd messed up both their lives and put his lover in danger. Moving them to Earth had confused and upset Alec, and even after John explained the collectors' agenda, Alec hadn't really understood.

Until now.

John's body still tingled from their lovemaking. Even though he'd longed for both Alec and Tara, a part of him had never believed it would happen. He'd been so relieved to see Alec and Tara form a close bond that he'd been willing just to live his love for Tara vicariously through Alec, but to have her love him too was a gift he would never undervalue. He just hoped she still felt the same way after Alec told her the complete ugly truth on how they ended up living in a cave in the middle of nowhere.

He tried to swallow against the emotion clogging his throat. He had no idea how he would live without them, but if that's what it took for them both to be happy, he'd find a way.

It took him much longer to pick up supplies and return to the cave than he intended, but when he got there, he found the place empty.

Chapter Eleven

Tara woke slowly, her confusion heightened by the fact that she seemed to be locked in a completely dark room. She moved her wrists only to find herself attached to a wall the same way John had secured her that first night.

She shook her head sharply. Were the last three weeks just a dream?

Hoping to get her bearings she blinked her eyes several times, trying to see the small LED display that had been in that little room. Nothing. There seemed to be no light of any kind, and the fear that she was actually blind started to seep through her.

She tried to speak several times, but her tongue and lips felt strange, felt numb. She tried again but could force no more than a low moan from her throat. What the hell was wrong with her?

Things felt surreal, almost like she floated outside her body, but at the same time like her skin was too tight. She rubbed her face and chest, the stinging, burning sensation just feeling worse. It took a few more minutes of trying to reach the skin on her back and shoulders before she realized that she was completely naked.

A bright light hit her eyes. She slammed them closed and pressed her face into her arms. A cruel laugh sounded off to her left, and she blinked rapidly, trying to adjust her vision so that she could see her tormentor.

Gasping for breath, Tara squinted against the harsh light but could only make out rough features of the man in front of her. He laughed again, and the violent urge to lodge his balls deep in his throat buzzed through her. If only he'd step a little closer. She didn't give a fuck who he was. The bastard deserved pain simply for that mocking laugh.

"Not so tough now?" he asked in English. "I had to promise Grieg first allocation just so he wouldn't retaliate. You sure made a mess of his face."

He laughed again, but she hung her head lower, straining to remember. She had blurred images of a fight, fuzzy memories of elbowing someone, of Alec's deep voice. She closed her eyes, the images gray and watery, her recollection poor and incomplete.

She tried to talk, tried to ask what they'd done to Alec, but if felt like her tongue was too big for her mouth, and the words came out sounding like grunts. She growled low in her throat in frustration, and the man in front of her laughed even louder.

"Kind of hard to use that smart mouth now that the drugs are kicking in, huh?" He said it in such a smug voice she wanted to kick the bastard again. She was pretty sure he was the one she managed to double over with a well-placed foot, but considering her current situation, it obviously hadn't been hard enough.

He stepped closer, and she lashed out with her foot, but even her coordination felt off, and she missed completely. He grabbed her by the hair and bent her backwards so that her entire weight dragged against her bound wrists. He leaned closer to smile into her face and then said words that chilled her to the bone. "Don't you just love these drugs? You get to understand every word, every emotion, every action but can't do a thing to control it. I love watching you humans get what you deserve, but I'm especially going to enjoy watching you get yours. Grieg is going to make sure you never forget who he is."

Tara tried to pull away, but he pulled harder on her hair until she cried out in pain. "That's it, bitch. We're gonna hear a whole lot more of that moaning before we let you get pregnant."

He released her, and she fell to her knees. Tara felt like she was crying, but the drugs in her system made her unsure of anything. Her vision blurred, and she rubbed her face frantically, the stinging itch feeling worse with every moment.

"Now, now, we can't have you messing up that pretty face."

Tara rubbed harder, lifting to her feet as her arms were pulled high above her head. Desperately, she began rubbing the inflamed skin against her upper arms, whatever part of her she could reach, but he stepped closer, adjusted her bonds slightly, and then she felt her arms pulled in separate directions. Before she understood what was happening, her feet were locked into cuffs, as well, and she stood spread-eagle against the wall. She moaned again as the need to claw at her burning skin engulfed her.

"Just wait until the itch makes it to your pussy. You'll want a hard cock in there so bad you won't even care who it belongs to." He patted her cheek, and she almost rubbed against the rough skin of his hand. She managed to stop herself at the last moment, but the need clawed at her insides. "But you get to wait until John can see what happens when he breaks the rules. You and Alec are going to serve as an example to the rest of the crew of what could happen to their loved ones if they break their oath."

She tried to turn away from him, his words lancing deep into her soul. John had tried to protect them both, and now he would be forced to watch whatever they planned for her and Alec. She felt tears roll down the inflamed skin on her cheeks as she realized how badly it would destroy John to witness the very thing he'd tried to stop from happening. He would surely blame himself for getting Alec involved.

She heard the door slam closed as her tormentor left. She tried to suck in a deep breath, tried to find a small center of calm, tried not to moan as the heat traveled down her torso, and her knees buckled. Her full weight hung on her wrists for a moment before everything tilted. At first she thought she was losing consciousness, and a cowardly part welcomed the promised relief, but a moment later her back pressed against the cool metal wall, and she realized that the wall had slanted almost to a horizontal position.

She sobbed harder as she realized that unlike that first night John had abducted her, this time there was no misunderstanding. These men, these aliens, meant her harm, and under the drug's influence, she was helpless to stop it.

* * * *

John wandered through the camping equipment, at first fearing that Tara had left simply because she feared him and his past. A quick search of the area showed signs of a struggle, and his fear ramped into absolute terror. They had her. They had Alec.

"About time you showed," a familiar voice said from behind him.

"Altan, where are they? What did you do with them?" John was wishing he hadn't left without at least putting his pistol into his pocket. He never went anywhere without it, but he'd been in such a hurry to leave when Tara had started asking about what happened to the women they captured that he'd broken one of his most sacred rules—never be unarmed.

"Relax," Altan said tiredly. The man held a stun gun pointed at John's chest, so he doubted relaxing was possible at this point.

"What are you waiting for?" John asked aggressively, trying to put Altan off, trying to cover the fact that he was circling toward the work bench where he keep his tools, hoping to find something he could use as a weapon.

"I'm waiting for you to relax so that we can talk."

"Talk? What's to talk about? You're here to arrest me and take me back to the ship. Seems to me that doesn't require a whole lot of talking." He continued to inch toward the bench, hoping that his belligerent attitude would cover his true purpose. He had to find a way to get Tara and Alec back, and the only way he was going to be able to do that is if he avoided capture himself.

"We could talk about why you did it. Why you risked everything to protect a human. We could talk about how you can't find the parts you need to make a dampening field small enough to hide her. Or how about the fact that the breeding council has known exactly where you've been hiding for the past six months." John felt his mouth fall open.

"How?" Words weren't coming easily, his brain spinning with what-ifs.

"Pure dumb luck," he said shrugging. "That little asshole, Grieg, spotted you on our last collection mission. Once the council knew where you were, they just waited for you to lead them to Tara. I expect that her abduction will be a far worse experience now that they plan to make an example of you."

John couldn't quite hide his terror, and he inched closer to the bench behind him. "Or maybe," Altan continued, "we could talk about how lucky you are that they left me behind to apprehend you."

"Lucky?" John asked sarcastically.

"Yes, lucky. I know where Tara and Alec are, and I have a plan to get them back."

John shook his head in bewilderment. "Why would you help me?"

"Because you're not the only one who thinks what is happening is wrong. You're not the only one to see that human women are intelligent, and you are sure as hell not the only one to try and change the ways things are. You are, however, the only one who has managed to hide a breeder from them for so long." Altan lowered his pistol and then dropped into the nearest chair.

"I've been a collector for twelve Earth years. I've stood by helplessly and watched as intelligent human women are reduced to nothing but mindless slaves. At first I tried to justify it. Tried to convince myself that we were saving our species, but when I learned that the women retain their cognitive abilities even while the drugs are at their peak, I couldn't stand by and do nothing any longer."

Oh hell, that was something John didn't know. He'd always thought that the drugs affected the women's minds as well. He hadn't known they retained enough understanding to know what was happening. John needed to do something, needed to move, needed to save his lovers, but he also needed Altan's help. So he stood there, his muscles tensed, his breathing choppy as he listened to his former shipmate explain his plan.

Chapter Twelve

Alec woke with one hell of a headache. He barely remembered why his head hurt until he tried to move his hand to his face. The cuffs holding his hands in place bought it all flooding back. He closed his eyes as the horrifying scene replayed in his head.

They'd been asleep, curled together, when he heard a noise at the cave opening. He'd barely rolled off the bed when a stun shot hit him, and he went down hard.

Tara fought them, lashing out with her fists and feet, and he'd smiled when he heard one of them grunt in groin-mangled agony. Alec had almost overcome the effects of the stun shot when a second shot hit him in the lower back. Tara shrieked, and he felt her slight weight wrap over his prone form protectively.

"No," she screamed as the men moved toward him. "I'll come with you, just…just leave him alone. He's innocent. He has nothing to do with this."

He heard a familiar laugh but struggled to place it. One of John's shipmates? He'd met a few before they'd left for John's first assignment but couldn't remember all their names. Grieg, maybe? He wasn't certain, but he sure sounded like that prick. The guy was a nasty little asshole with a vicious streak, and Alec had hated him even before they'd had a full conversation.

"Innocent? Is that so?" Grieg said, sounding amused. It had to be him. The tone of voice was exactly the same. "Innocent? Such an interesting word. I suppose you expect me to let him go." The other men laughed, and he felt Tara hug him tighter.

"Just leave him here. He's not a threat to you."

Alec felt someone step closer to them and lift Tara off his back. She grabbed his shoulders, desperately holding on as she whispered, "Don't risk coming for me. I love you both."

His chest tightened with anguish. She was willing to sacrifice herself in the hopes of saving the next woman. She would willingly leave John and Alec behind if it meant keeping them safe. God, he loved this woman. His species was so wrong, so misguided. Couldn't they see that human women should be valued and cherished, not used and destroyed?

"Oh such lovely heartfelt sentiments," Grieg said mockingly. "So I guess it won't hurt, then, to offer your innocent friend Alec a ride. He is, after all, a very long way from home."

"No," she yelled angrily.

Alec heard a grunt and managed to turn his head in time to see Grieg hit the ground, his face bloodied, his nose looking broken. Grim satisfaction drilled through him at the same time fear for what the man might do in retaliation chilled the blood in his veins.

"Enough," a commanding voice growled. "Get her back to the ship without damaging her. Sedate her if you have to."

Alec closed his eyes as he heard Tara's struggles come to an end. He prayed they'd only sedated her, but from his prone position he could no longer see where she was.

"When John catches up with you," Alec mumbled, "you will regret the day you were born." He heard an amused chuckle at the same time something warm pressed against his neck, and unconsciousness claimed him.

The sound of a door opening bought him back to his current predicament. He smirked when he saw Grieg's messed-up face. "Like that do you?" Grieg said as he stalked closer. "Well, it's nothing compared to what I'm going to do to that whore once the hormone treatment is finished."

Alec's fists rose of their own accord, but the tether held him back, and Grieg laughed even harder. "Don't worry, Alec. You and John are going to have front row seats."

Alec bit back the groan of agony that twisted his gut, fear for both his lovers stabbing through every part of his body.

He knew it was coming but could do nothing to avoid it without angering Grieg further. The punch landed hard against his nose, the pain exploding out and up across his eyes and cheekbones. He tasted blood but did nothing to retaliate. With his arms bound, he had little hope of doing any more than making this fun for Grieg, so he hung his head low, the actions of a conquered man even as his mind raced with thoughts.

Mistaking Alec's posture as defeat, Grieg stepped closer and unwittingly gave Alec the opportunity he'd prayed for. Moving fast, Alec used every bit of strength he had to kick Grieg straight in the groin. The man hit the floor hard, coughing and moaning as he held his balls and curled into himself. Alec didn't care what the bastard did to him, but he prayed he'd done enough damage to keep the sadistic prick away from Tara for a very long time.

"Grieg, what the fuck are you doing? We were told to guard the prisoner, not torture him." The second man to enter the room glanced over at Alec with an annoyed look on his face and then turned his attention to his injured comrade. "Get back to your guard station before a supervisor comes in." The man lifted Grieg to his feet, completely disregarding the other man's obvious pain. It would seem that Alec wasn't the only one to draw satisfaction from the well-aimed kick.

* * * *

"Permission to dock granted," the voice said through the transport pod's speakers. Within moments the main ship took over the controls of the small craft and guided it into the hangar bay.

"Okay, once we land I'm going to follow orders, transport you to the holding cell, and then check in with my men. I need to know where Tara and Alec are being held before we can put any rescue plan into action."

"How do I know I can trust you?" John asked angrily. He didn't like this situation one little bit. He only had Altan's word that he could be trusted, and quite frankly after everything that had happened recently, any man's word didn't seem enough.

"You don't know," he said seriously. "But at this point you have no choice. Either you follow my plan, or you abandon Tara and Alec to their fates." He shrugged. "Your choice."

God, John wanted to smash something. How could the man be so damn calm? He was talking about smuggling two prisoners off a heavily fortified collector ship full of armed guards.

"How long will it take to find them?"

"John, I don't know. Look, you trusted me enough to get on this transport, now trust me enough to get the job done."

John nodded in resignation. The man was right. They were on a course of action, and he had little choice but to follow it now.

"Okay," John said quietly.

He held his arms out so that Altan could secure the wrist restraints. "Now remember to stay calm. I've told them that I sedated you, so they are expecting you to be bound but compliant. Follow their orders like a sleepwalker." John nodded his understanding just as they felt the air pressure valves release.

Within moments two heavily armed guards stepped into the cabin and grabbed his arms. He did as Altan had instructed and walked between them as if he were still asleep. His heart rate kicked into overdrive when the cell door slammed closed, but he took a deep breath and tried to convince himself he'd done the only thing he could to save his family.

* * * *

Tara squirmed against her bonds. If she got any hotter, she felt like she'd burst into flames—spontaneous human combustion, alien style. All over she felt swollen, itchy, aching. She whimpered in need as her pussy contracted, fisting around nothing. Her clit throbbed. The little bud was so swollen and tender now that it had pushed passed the protective hood.

Tears flowed down the sides of her face as she moaned in agony. Now that she understood what John had been trying to save her from, her heart ached all the more for the man who'd given up everything to protect her.

The door slid open, and she heard two voices, one familiar and one new.

"Yes, Altan," the familiar voice said, "we've prepared her as ordered. She'll be ready for impregnation activities within a few hours."

"Excellent. Prepare the viewing room. The Seniors wish to witness this one's training. They've decided to make her an example of what happens when collectors fail to do their duty as ordered."

Tara tried to bite her lip to stop the whimper from escaping, but it was no use. The drugs overruled her brain, and she gasped as a callused hand slid gently up her leg and closer to her pussy. The fingers swirled in the juices that leaked onto her thighs as a masculine chuckle filled the room.

"Yes, this one is nearly ready. I look forward to watching her beg."

Tara wanted to growl, wanted to swear and rage at the man, but the only thing that left her throat was another soft whimper as the hand withdrew. She pressed her heels harder against the platform, straining to lift her pussy toward the withdrawing fingers even as she screamed hatred in her mind.

God help her. Death seemed preferable to this torture, but the moment the thought crossed her mind, she discarded it completely. Alec was here somewhere. John would come for them both.

She just prayed she'd be able to survive whatever Grieg had planned long enough for John to rescue them.

Chapter Thirteen

Alec sat of the floor, his arms lifted over his head as the tether pulled tight. His nose ached, his face felt puffy and swollen, and it was only possible to breathe through his mouth, but at least the bleeding had stopped.

He kept his head low as the door opened and several booted feet walked toward him. "Who did this?" an angry voice asked.

"Um…he…um," a voice mumbled.

"Speak up," the other voice commanded.

"Grieg did, sir."

"Where is Grieg now?"

"In the infirmary, s…sir. The prisoner managed to kick him pretty hard in the um…after Grieg broke his nose."

A quiet chuckle broke the tension. "Rather effective disciplinary action wouldn't you say?"

"Yes, sir," the younger voice said, sounding confused.

"Go inform Grieg that he will be removed from the allocation list immediately and suspended from duties until further notice. Send one of the medical technicians to heal this man's injuries."

"Yes, sir." The young guard sounded relieved to be able to leave, and for just a small moment Alec felt sorry for him. He'd been the one to stop Grieg's attack, so it proved that not all of the collectors were rabid animals like Grieg.

Alec tried to swallow the thick mucus clogging his mouth as he waited for the new person to speak. It felt like ages, but finally the man moved toward him, and a part of Alec wondered if he should brace for another blow. The man had certainly made sure he had no witnesses, and despite the man's anger at what Grieg had done to him, Alec was not about to trust this stranger.

"Alec, do you know who I am?" Alec lifted his head, trying to make out the man's features through his swollen eyelids. A callused hand touched the side of his face gently. "We met a few years ago at John's graduation party. I'm Altan." Alex nodded his head, not really sure that he did remember the man or not but willing to go along with anything if it would delay another beating. "I'm here with John to rescue you and Tara, but we need to get you medical attention before I risk blowing my cover."

"John?" he mumbled, anxious to know what was going on.

"He's safe. I've located Tara, and I'll come back for you as soon as I can." There was a noise in the hallway, and Altan stepped back quickly. Alec hung his head again his mind racing with possibilities. "Good. Heal this man's injuries. I'll be back to take him to the allocation ceremony shortly."

Allocation ceremony? He could only be talking about Tara. The allocation ceremonies were usually held on the planet. The only reason he could think of to perform one on the ship was to teach everyone on board what happens to anyone who tries to circumvent their authority.

Shit! That meant Tara was already being pumped full of fertility drugs. His hands shook as he tried not to think about how frightened Tara would be right now. The technician healed his injuries without commenting on how hard Alec shook. Anger rolled through him as he tried to draw in deep breaths and waited for Altan to return. If he returned.

* * * *

The longer it took, the more anxious John became. If it had been possible, he would've paced his cell like a caged lion. He wanted to growl his frustration and was ready to do anything—bribe, beg, promise the world just to get the chance to save Tara and Alec.

The door slid open, and Altan and a uniformed guard stepped through. The guard hurried to undo the bindings holding John prisoner and then stepped back and let Altan talk. "This is Beiltar. He's going to help you rescue Tara while I get Alec to a transport."

John nodded. "What's the plan?" he asked as he rubbed his aching wrists.

"The allocation ceremony is scheduled to start soon. You are supposed to be chained to the wall and forced to watch." John's blood ran cold at the same time anger pumped heat through his heart. They weren't even going to transport her back to the planet before they began their abuse.

"Wait," John said. "Does that mean they've already drugged her?"

Altan nodded grimly. "She is already in the final stages. We need to move quickly."

Every muscle, every nerve ending pulsed with the need to rush in and save Tara, but he managed to rein in his emotions, barely. Tara needed him to act with a clear head. If he failed her now, there wouldn't be another chance.

"Beiltar has been assigned to escort you to the viewing area. Fortunately, the path he needs to take passes where Tara is being held. You'll probably have to overpower the guards, but between the two of you it should be fairly simple."

John nodded his understanding as another thought occurred to him. "We need to grab some technology, too. I can build a portable field dampener, but I haven't been able to find the materials on Earth. If we can't hide Tara, they'll just come for her again."

Altan was already nodding his agreement before he'd even finished the thought. "I'll detour via the weapons locker. We're going to need them on the transport anyway, so I'll grab some of the scanners as well. Do they contain the materials you need?"

"Yes," John answered quietly as they stepped through the open doorway and went their separate ways.

* * * *

Tara was beyond terrified. It was like her body no longer belonged to her, like she wasn't the one controlling her limbs. She tried to scream when she heard the door slide open, but it sounded more like a moan to her ears.

She opened her eyes to find John standing beside her, trying to loosen the cuffs around her ankles. But she knew it wasn't John. It couldn't be. Her mind and the drugs were tricking her, showing her the thing she wanted most. No doubt the other man would look exactly like Alec. She didn't even want to look. She knew what she was seeing wasn't real, so why torture herself with the hope.

As soon as her legs were released she squeezed them closed, rubbing her slippery thighs together, trying to find relief to the overwhelming need that the drugs induced. In her head she vowed to fight them, promised herself that she would resist the need, but even as she thought the words, she knew it wasn't true. The drugs had robbed her of her self-control, and she had no chance of following through on her anger.

"Tara." John's voice reached her ears, and she squeezed her eyes closed in anguish. Would every alien allocated to impregnate her appear as either John or Alec? Would she be forced to endure the drugs' effects with men wearing her lovers' faces?

"Tara, baby, please look at me." She shook her head hard, surprised that she had even that much control. As soon as her arms were released, her hands went straight to her pussy, her fingers slipping over her aching clit, her fingers pressing into her dripping slit. She moaned at the relief and the agony and vowed retribution to all involved.

"No, baby. You're going to hurt yourself." Gentle hands gripped her wrists, and she tugged against the hold, trying to find relief, trying to find an end to the torment. "Tara, I'm going to take you home, baby. You just need to hold on a little longer."

Such beautiful words. Every part of her wanted to believe that this really was John, but to give in the temptation to believe made her foolish. She gasped as she was gathered into strong arms and held against a muscled chest. Another man stepped closer, and between the two of them, they managed to wrap her in some type of material, effectively immobilizing her. She whimpered at the return to imprisonment, but some part of her also realized that she could do some serious damage by her own actions in this state of sexual frenzy.

Just a little bit grateful, Tara opened her eyes expecting to see Alec's kind face. There was no mistaking this man for Alec. She twisted her head, startled to find the man holding her still looked like John. Was it possible it was him?

She tried to say his name, but the words came out wrong, and she started to cry even harder with frustration. Strong arms squeezed her tighter.

"Don't cry, baby. We'll be home soon."

She wanted desperately to believe this man was John, so she nodded her head against his chest and closed her eyes against the tears.

Chapter Fourteen

"Alec," Altan said as he stepped through the doorway. "We need to move quickly."

"Tara?" he asked, his worry for her safety overriding everything else in his mind.

"John has her. They'll meet us at the transport shortly, but you and I have another mission first."

Alec tilted his head and looked at Altan expectantly, but the older man just handed him a weapon and headed out the door. Alec glanced at the weapon in his hand, hoping that he wouldn't have to use it. The fact that he had no idea how to use it could be a major problem.

Quietly, Alec followed Altan as they made their way through the corridors. Alec wasn't familiar with this ship at all, and several times he felt like they'd traveled in a complete circle. Finally, they came to a security door. Altan stunned the only guard on duty and then unlocked the door and stepped inside. Alec followed quickly, dragging the guard into the room, unwilling to get caught loitering in the hallway.

"Jade, are you okay?" Altan asked the naked human woman tethered to the wall by her wrists.

She nodded and shook her head at the same time, and Alec figured that pretty much summed up the way he was feeling, too. Altan undid her restraints and handed her his coat. The jacket practically covered her from neck to knee, but as she stepped forward, she stumbled a little, and Altan pulled her into his arms for a moment while she found her balance.

"I'm okay," she said quietly. Altan touched her face with his large hand, his fingers trembling slightly as he breathed deeply. Then he grabbed her hand and headed for the door.

* * * *

"Where are they?" John asked in agitation. He and Tara and Beiltar had reached the hangar bay without incident. The entire ship was practically deserted, and Beiltar had explained that all crew had been ordered to the viewing area so that they could not only witness the allocation ceremony but also the punishment meted out to collectors who thought to circumvent the breeding council's authority.

Beiltar didn't hint at what John's punishment may have been, but John knew the breeding council well enough to know it wouldn't have been pleasant. He held Tara in his arms as she continued to writhe with the drugs' effects.

Tears misted his vision as she moaned again, the sound unpleasant and animalistic, not the sound of a woman in the throes of desire. Her eyes continued to dart around the area as if she had little control over where they landed or what they saw.

Beiltar signaled to him to keep quiet as they heard the approach of hurried footsteps. Tara moaned, and he pressed his lips to hers to swallow the sound of her agony. She kissed him back enthusiastically, but he tried to keep the contact brief and light. Tara had no control over her body, and he would never abuse the trust she'd placed in him only a few days earlier.

Beiltar stepped out of the transport craft, and John held his breath as he waited for either his return or the sounds of a fight. Neither happened, but the next person to walk through the door filled his heart and soul with such relief that he almost cried out his name.

Alec saw him, carefully placed the heavy sack he'd been carrying on the floor, and hurried to him and Tara. He kissed Tara on the forehead, his look of relief warring with the same anguish John felt. He leaned forward to press a kiss to John's mouth.

"Is she okay?" he asked quietly.

"She'll be fine as soon as the drugs wear off." John knew it was more complicated than that but didn't want to add to Alec's worries at the moment. There would be plenty of time to worry about Tara's recovery once they escaped the ship.

"We managed to grab some weapons and supplies. Would it be okay to give Tara a sedative?"

Relief coursed through John. "Yes."

Alec dragged the sack of supplies over to John. It looked like they'd practically cleaned out one of the medical storage lockers. He spotted a sedation rod easily, and Alec handed it to him to administer. Almost immediately, Tara sighed quietly and slipped into a fitful sleep, but at least she wasn't screaming in frustration.

Beiltar stepped back into the ship with a young woman pressed against him. She looked about the same age as Tara but smaller, more fragile, but at least she didn't seem to be drugged.

"Altan?" John asked Beiltar as the door slid closed. Beiltar shook his head. "He's staying undercover. He hopes he can find more like us and maybe put a stop to collections." John nodded his understanding, realizing there was a whole lot more to the story. "We have five Earth minutes before Altan sounds the alarm. He's headed to Tara's cell as we speak." The small transport lifted off the ground and swung around to face the closed hangar bay door. The word "How?" was on the tip of John's tongue, but he quickly swallowed it when a flash and small amount of smoke caused the doors to blow outwards.

"Well timed," John said admiring Beiltar's handy work.

"Thanks," he said as he flew the little ship through the opening and into space. John noticed with surprise that they were still in orbit around Earth.

"Are there still collectors on the planet?"

"Not at the moment, but they plan to resume as soon as…well, I suppose they'll resume after all the fallout from your escape now."

"Any idea where we can hide while I get the portable dampening fields built."

Beiltar smiled seeming more relaxed now that they were moving. "Ever heard of Coober Pedy?" John shook his head. "It's a small outback town in Australia. Many of the buildings are underground. The locals call them dugouts, and they even have some that are luxury hotels. I figure if we stay a few weeks underground while we make the portable field dampeners, we should be able to avoid their scans at least until their next collection expedition."

"Local currency?" John asked, concerned over the practicalities.

"Taken care of. Altan made sure that I have enough money to last several lifetimes on this planet. Spending a few dollars on a luxury resort is not going to be a problem, and besides, after everything you've been through in the last few weeks, I think you three are entitled to a little comfort."

John glanced down at the woman sleeping in his arms. She deserved comfort and a whole lot more, and as soon as the drugs wore off, he was going to make sure both his lovers knew how important they were to him.

Chapter Fifteen

Tara growled in frustration.

"John, I'm fine. Really, the drugs wore off days ago." For five wonderful, glorious, frustrating days Alec and John had held her and soothed her and comforted her as the drugs worked out of her system.

It had taken nearly two days before she'd been able to use her voice, and she'd spent a lot of time since then trying to reassure them both that she was okay. Unfortunately, they'd taken her attempts to cuddle into them as a sign that the drugs still ruled her choices and had sedated her several more times before she'd been able to convince them not to.

Quite a few times, both John and Alec had soothed her overwrought body by gently sucking and licking her clit until she reached orgasm, but neither man had penetrated her. Now, three days after she got her voice back, they still refused to do anything more than hold her.

Well, she'd just about had enough of their coddling, and things were going to change right now!

"Alec, tell him I'm fine."

Alec smiled that sexy, gorgeous smile, and excitement zipped through her midsection. She knew he was convinced, but she also knew he wouldn't make love to her until John believed her, too.

She lifted away from the bed and slipped the buttons of her shirt open as she sashayed toward John. His eyes darkened, and his nostrils flared as she got closer, but he shook his head even as he pulled her into his embrace. Despite the fact that she'd promised herself that she wouldn't do it, she growled in frustration as he pressed her face against his heart.

"I know you're okay, baby. Alec and I are very glad you're feeling better." She rubbed her face against his chest, enjoying the warm feeling that always came from his embrace. "We just want to be certain that you are making your own decisions and not influenced by the drugs still."

"I am making my own decisions." She wasn't really impressed with the sulky tone of her voice, but it had been a long week and she really needed to feel attraction and desire that wasn't drug induced. She wanted to feel real love and real emotion for both her men. "John, I wasn't under the drugs influence when we made love in the caves." He stilled at her spoken words, so she rushed on, trying to explain what she felt. "I need to be with you, love you, and watch you and Alec love each other. I need to feel normal."

"Oh, baby," he said sorrow softening his voice. "I'm just trying to protect you. I want you to know that Alec and I would never do anything you didn't want us to do."

She smiled, shamelessly taking advantage of the opening he'd just delivered her.

"Well, I don't want you to *not* make love to me."

Alec's strong chuckle sounded behind her, and she felt John's chest shake with suppressed laughter. "Okay, Tara," Alec said finally. "I think maybe we can convince him with a little work." He leaned over her and kissed John reverently, gently trapping Tara between them. "What do you say, big guy? Ready to ravish your lovers?"

John grinned, leaned forward, and lifted Tara over his shoulder. She giggled as he caressed her bottom and moaned when he squeezed the soft flesh with his big hand. He lowered her to the bed, kissing her gently as he finished undoing the buttons on her shirt and pushed it open. She wasn't wearing a bra, so her beaded nipples crinkled even tighter when she saw the heat in his eyes.

Alec crawled onto the bed behind John and set to work relieving them all of clothing. Inch by gorgeous inch, the men of her dreams—and her heart and her reality—were revealed to her avid gaze. She licked her lips as she lifted her face to John's mouth. He kissed her like she was fragile, precious, and her heart constricted at the care and restraint Alec and John had shown over the past few days. One of them had been with her constantly since they'd escaped the ship, so she knew that they hadn't even had a chance to be together.

Finally divested of clothing, John groaned as Alec wrapped his hand around his hard cock, pumping the tumescent flesh with his fist. John leaned forward, chasing Tara with his kisses as she fell back onto the mattress. She moaned into his mouth as Alec urged him to cover her body with his own. She was already dripping wet with want, but John skimmed her clit with his fingers, dipping lower to her hot core, making certain that he wouldn't hurt her.

Her eyes misted as he pressed his thick cock into her tender flesh with such exquisite care. She loved that about him. He'd never hurt her. Several times over the last few days, she'd thought about that moment almost a month ago when he'd slammed into her home and abducted her. It had taken a little while to reconcile her feelings. Even as it had been happening, her instinct had been to trust him, but fear had overridden her thought processes. She knew now without a shadow of a doubt that he was an honorable man and that her intuition had been spot on. Her only regret was that she hadn't realized sooner. She had no doubt that her behavior that day, her fear and mistrust, had hurt him deeply, and she was prepared to spend the rest of her life making it up to him, convincing him that he did the only thing he could've done under the circumstances.

He pressed farther into her but seemed to lose control for a moment and forced his cock deeper. She gasped as it happened again, and she heard Alec's reassuring voice.

"Shhh, it's okay, John. Let me and Tara take care of you this time."

* * * *

John flinched away from the unexpected contact, forcing his cock deeper into Tara's warm pussy. She gasped, and he hesitated until he realized she'd gasped in arousal, not in pain.

Alec's quiet words filled him with liquid warmth. Alec had never topped him, so the cold lubricant had been a shock. The finger swirling around the rim of his anus had him groaning from the exquisite sensations. His muscles jumped as each new feeling teased his senses.

He kissed Tara with abandon as a single finger pressed past the tight muscle and breached his ass. A second finger followed, Alec setting a gentle pace as he stretched the muscle to take his cock. John drilled into Tara and on each withdrawal pushed onto the fingers, forcing them deeper into his body.

"Alec," he pleaded. A strong arm wrapped around his waist as the fingers withdrew, replaced quickly by the head of Alec's cock.

"I love you," Alec whispered into his ear as his cock stretched him and slid into his ass inch by excruciatingly slow inch. John pushed back against the cock sliding deeper into his channel as he gasped for breath. The sensation was incredible. He'd hoped that Alec would do this for him one day. He just hadn't expected that day to be this one.

Tara watched him, a smile curving across her face. "I love you," she said.

He kissed her, trying to hold his weight off her as Alec picked up the pace and began slamming into his ass again and again. The amazing sensations multiplied. With his cock nestled in Tara's heavenly warmth, his ass filled to the brim with his lover's hard rod, John could no longer control himself. He pumped into Tara, one hand supporting his weight while the other grabbed her hip and held her still for his taking. Then he pushed back onto Alec's hard cock, impaling himself on that hard rod.

Back and forth. Back and forth. Each movement more exquisite, more thrilling, more amazing. Tara cried out as her orgasm gripped his cock tighter. Heat blasted through him as he erupted, his hot seed pulsing deep into her welcoming flesh. He squeezed his ass as Alec's cock swelled and throbbed. A moment later Alec's climax claimed him.

Alec hugged him close, his entire exhausted weight pressing down on him. John had never felt more loved, and the feeling only increased when he realized that Tara and Alec had their fingers entwined. They'd held on to each other even as they'd shown him he was loved and valued.

Alec kissed the back of his neck and slowly extricated his softening cock. "Stay," he ordered.

That was one order John was happy to follow. He wasn't sure his legs were working yet anyway. Carefully he lowered himself onto the bed beside Tara. She smiled into his eyes and told him again that she loved him.

"I love you, sweet Tara. I have for a long time."

"I'm sorry I hurt you that first day." Even before she finished the sentence he was shaking his head.

"Don't ever apologize for being frightened. If I'd handled things differently, maybe I could've saved you from that."

She placed her fingers over his mouth and shook her head. "Thank you for everything. Scaring me that first day was far preferable to what could've happened. Looking back now, I know a part of me wanted to trust you."

Alec came back into the room, quickly cleaned them both up, and lay down on Tara's other side. He propped his head on his hand and drew lazy circles on Tara's belly.

"Feel better?" he asked with a big grin on his face.

"Much better," Tara answered shyly.

"Hey," Alec said, his fingers caressing her chin. "What's that look for?"

She blushed, that wonderful blush that traveled from the roots of her hair to the tips of her toes. "I was just thinking," she mumbled. "Is there a chance I could still be fertile from the drugs?"

"No," John answered quickly, his heart contracting just a little that she would ask. She said she loved him, but it seemed she still didn't trust him to protect her. "Pregnancy is only possible while you are on the drugs. There is no residual effect once they are out of your system."

She looked disappointed, and he couldn't understand why.

"Tara?" Alec asked her, looking as bewildered as John felt.

"I was just wondering, if, well one day when things are safer, when we have a home and somewhere to raise them, if you'd maybe consider having a baby with me, starting a family." She'd gone almost florescent pink by the time she finished hurrying the words past her lips.

John couldn't deny the appeal of having a baby with the two people most important to him, but he'd never ask Tara to go through the hormone therapy ever again. The last few days had been absolutely harrowing, and he didn't even want to consider putting her through such an experience on purpose.

"No." He shook his head. "No, no way. I'll never ask you to go through that again. Don't you remember how bad it was?"

"Yes, it was bad, but I trust you and Alec to protect me."

"No. Absolutely not. I won't allow it."

Oh, such a bad thing to say to his woman. He knew Tara hated being told what to do, but this was one subject he refused to compromise. She pushed herself to a sitting position and crossed her arms over those delicious breasts. It was obvious she was beyond angry, but the thing that hit him hardest was the hurt in her eyes.

Alec moved quickly to pull her into his arms. He also glared at John like he'd grown two heads.

"Tara, honey. It's not safe on Earth for any of us yet, but I know that we can find a way to get you pregnant without putting you at risk."

Tara lifted her tear-stained face to Alec's, a look of such hope on her lovely features that John wanted to pull her into his embrace and promise her anything. Instead, he directed his anger at Alec.

"No. Don't promise things you can't deliver." He couldn't sit still any longer. He had to move, had to do something, had to keep a level head and make the sane choices for his family. Why Alec would even consider it was beyond John's comprehension. Tara had just spent days in absolute agony. How could either of them even consider putting her through that again?

"John," Alec said quietly, his voice calm, his tone reasonable. "I spoke to Beiltar. He used to work in the medical labs on the ship. He thinks there is a way to separate the fertility treatment from the drugs that affect speech and behavior."

"Really?" John asked rather stupidly. Alec wouldn't have said it if it wasn't true, but the unexpected hope overflowing his heart was a real surprise to John. He sat on the bed and reached a hand over to Tara's cheek. He caught the tear that leaked from her eye and then leaned forward to kiss her gently. "Baby, we need to be patient, but if we can make the treatment safe for you, then we'll consider it. We need to make sure that you're hidden from their scans first, but then we'll figure something out. I would really love for the three of us to have children."

She surprised him by crying harder. Alec looked at him, a reflection of his own confusion.

"Baby, please don't cry."

"I'm not crying," she said in a watery voice. Again he glanced at Alec, and again he saw only confusion. She hiccupped, and a small laugh escaped her even as the tears continued to fall. "I thought you didn't want me. I thought you didn't want to have a family with me."

"Oh, sweet Tara, you are our family *and* the center of our universe. We'll talk to Beiltar." She looked so happy he almost didn't want to say the rest, but keeping his family safe was his first priority. "When I'm sure the personal dampening fields and false signal generators are working properly, and we are in a safe situation, then we'll think about making babies."

She wriggled out of Alec's hold and moved to straddle John's lap. His cock rose to the occasion, and she smiled as she stroked him. "Promise?" she asked.

"Yes, I promise, but you have to promise to be patient. I need to keep you and Alec and any babies we may have safe from the collectors."

She nodded enthusiastically. "I agree one hundred percent. Safety first, then babies." She wrapped her arms around him and held on tight. "I love you."

Alec pressed up against her back, sliding his arms around them both. "I love you, too," he said quietly as his hand slipped around to grasp John's cock and guide it into Tara's warm, wet pussy.

* * * *

Tara held on tight as Alec carefully eased John onto his back, helping her to adjust to the new position without John's cock slipping from her body. Alec kissed the back of her neck and then pressed her shoulders down lower so that her ass pointed into the air.

"Baby, I want to fuck this sweet ass," he said, gently stroking the soft globes, his fingers grazing over the sensitive pucker. She gasped as she nodded. "Say it, baby. Say it out loud for me."

"I want you to fuck my ass. I want you both inside me. Please, Alec," she pleaded breathlessly as she squirmed against John's hold on her hips. She jumped at the first touch of Alec's slippery fingers, the lubricant colder than she expected. He teased her, swirling his fingers around and over the sensitive skin. Her ass tingled as a single thick finger pressed into the tight ring of muscle. He toyed with her, setting a gentle rhythm until she was pressing back against him, trying to force him deeper. A second finger joined the first, and her ass burned just a little, the sting adding to her excitement.

John held her still, his cock fully inside her pussy but not moving, and she wriggled, trying to get him to move. A third finger pressed into her ass, and she gasped as the burn filled her. For a moment she flashed back to the terror of the drugs, but John's large hand slid through her hair to cup the back of her head.

"Shhh, baby, we'll take care of you."

She smiled against his chest, the momentary fear forgotten, as he massaged her head in the same rhythm that Alec prepared her ass. She was whimpering with need by the time the fingers withdrew and Alec placed his cock at her entrance.

Alec pushed his cock into her rectum, gently working it in until his pelvis was pressed firmly against her ass cheeks. "Oh, God, I can feel you both," he said gasping for air, groaning loudly when John slowly slid his cock out of her pussy and carefully pressed back in.

Alec eased out of her slightly, sighing as he slid back in and John pulled out. They set a gentle rhythm, each man shaking slightly as they slowly, carefully increased the pace. Tara gasped with every thrust, moaned with every touch, and bucked when the sensations ratcheted much, much higher.

Her entire body throbbed as Alec's movements rubbed her clit against the coarse hair on John's pelvis. Again and again, the little nub pressed against him, each press, each touch sending bolts of sensation outward.

She gasped as heat burst through her body, wave after wave of heat rippling through her veins. She felt them both stop moving as her ass and pussy throbbed, sucking against them both as orgasm rushed through her and they found their own releases.

"I love you," she sighed as she practically melted onto John's chest.

She was almost asleep, both cocks deeply embedded in her body, when the phone jolted her from her lethargy. The only people who knew they were here were Jade and Beiltar, and she tried to move, worried for the other woman. Jade hadn't been drugged, but her experience hadn't been any more pleasant than her own.

"Hello," Alec mumbled into the receiver. "Excellent." He leaned forward and pressed a soft kiss to Tara's shoulder. "We'll be there soon." He hung up the phone and carefully extracted his cock from her ass.

She could feel John's tension and looked at him questioningly, but he was looking at Alec. "Yes?" he asked.

"Yes," Alec said happily. "Come on. Let's get cleaned up so we can see for ourselves."

"What?" Tara asked, annoyance at their cryptic attitude stealing her after-sex lethargy. "What's this all about?"

"Beiltar has managed to successfully calibrate the portable field dampeners and signal generators," Alec said as he lifted her into his arms. "You and Jade should be safe now. Even face-to-face, the scanners won't detect you. We might even be able to give you back your old life."

She shivered convulsively, unable to consider going back to that lonely existence. Alec hugged her tighter as he laughed quietly. "Should I take that as a sign that you don't want to go back to your old job?"

"Yes," she said, still shivering slightly. "I want to stay with you and John no matter where that leads me."

"No regrets?" John asked.

"None," she said happily, knowing it was true. She loved them both. Alien, human, it didn't matter. They loved her, she loved them, and they loved each other. Nothing on earth—or in the universe—would change that. Her world couldn't be more perfect.

Well maybe one tiny, little exception...a baby or two or three...and now that she would be hidden from the collectors' scans, she planned on working on that *exception* as soon as possible.

THE END

http://www.rachelclark.webs.com/

Siren Publishing

Ménage Amour

Their Taydelaan

Rachel Clark

THEIR TAYDELAAN

RACHEL CLARK
Copyright © 2011

Chapter One

Jade entered the hospital, a part of her cringing at the need for this visit. Kayla had sounded so excited on the phone, and Jade had smiled indulgently as her sister described Jessica and David's beautiful new baby. But when Kayla had slipped and described the child as her daughter, Jade had realized just how much of a fantasy her sister had been living.

She'd spent the last three hours in the car worrying for her sister's mental health. The fact that Kayla seemed to think she was in a loving relationship with a married couple had made it difficult for Jade to stay quiet. She'd only tried to talk to her sister once about it, but the conversation had deteriorated the way they usually did when they disagreed on something.

Jade squeezed past a group of people that seemed to be fawning over a young mother holding a wrapped baby in her arms. Every person was *ooohing* and *aaahing* over the small bundle, and Jade felt her heart clench just a little tighter. She'd accepted a long time ago that if the right man didn't come along soon that she'd never have a family of her own. She was okay with that—she really was—but happy little family scenes like that one were usually something she avoided.

Which is why this visit was doubly hard. Her sister was such a sweet person, and she deserved so much more than what the universe seemed inclined to give her. Hell, after the way one of her exes treated her, the woman should have enough karma points to live a long and happy life. But no, instead she'd somehow come to believe that a married couple loved her and that they would share their baby with her.

Trying not to look at the tiny bundle in the woman's arms, Jade didn't see the big guy until she slammed into him. "Sorry," she said instinctively, relieved to note that she'd walked into a tall, solid wall of muscle and not some frail new mother walking the corridors.

The man wrapped an arm around her middle, held her against him, and then smiled. She wanted to look away, but somehow she couldn't make her eyes obey. He raised his hand and dragged the knuckles down the side of her face in a move that felt very affectionate.

"Hello, beautiful," he said in a deep, sexy voice. Her previously dormant libido kicked in with surprising speed, and she gasped as she stared into the man's perfect face. He was the beautiful one—tall, sleek, muscular, with a smile to die for. Naughty fantasies played in her head even as she sucked in a horrified gasp of air.

Hell, for all she knew this guy was waiting for his wife to come out of the labor ward. Surprised and embarrassed at her willingness to be held by a complete stranger, Jade wriggled frantically to move away. After a moment's hesitation, he released his grip and let her stand on her own two feet.

"Ssssorry," she managed to force past lips that seemed unwilling to obey. She went to walk around the man, but he moved and stepped into her path.

"What's your name?" he asked, using that sexy smile to best effect.

Desire unraveled in her belly, and she had to swallow twice before she could even shake her head. She tried to step around him once more, but he moved again, apparently unwilling to let her pass. She shook her head anxiously as just a hint of fear wound through her brain. It'd been nearly a year, but it didn't stop the memory rising to the surface.

She took a deep breath, trying to control the rising panic. The man's head snapped back as if she'd hit him. The look he gave her seemed full of concern, but this time when she stepped around him, he let her go. She practically ran down the hallway, unconcerned about where she was going. She just needed to escape.

* * * *

Mitchell watched the woman as she hurried to the end of the hallway. Every instinct inside him screamed for him to follow her, but he'd felt her fear and didn't want to be the cause of more. The moment she'd fallen into his arms he'd been drawn to her in a way that hadn't happened since he'd met his partner Zachary. Just that brief touch had strengthened the link he'd felt with the woman, and now he could sense exactly where she was in the building.

He could also sense her distress. He barely held himself still, the instinct to go to her, to protect and comfort her, nearly overwhelming every other sensible thought in his head.

He had no idea how long he stood there, mentally tracking her movements after she'd turned the corner, but it wasn't until he felt Zack's telepathic touch in his mind that he roused enough to fully understand what had just happened.

"Everything okay?" Zack asked in a quiet telepathic voice. Mitchell nodded his head even though his lover wasn't in the same room. Thanks to their mate link, Zack would've felt everything Mitchell felt when he'd held the woman in his arms.

"I think you need to come down to the hospital." He smiled as he sent the words he'd often wondered if he'd ever get the chance to say. *"I just found our Taydelaan."*

* * * *

Fear was still thumping in her chest when Jade finally made it to the room where Kayla held a newborn baby girl in her arms. But something made her stop. Jade stood at the doorway, suddenly worried that she'd made the wrong decision. Kayla looked so content sitting there with a baby in her arms. Who was Jade to burst her delusional bubble?

But it wasn't her baby. The child wasn't her daughter. Genetically that just wasn't possible.

A quick glance at the bed showed Kayla's so-called partners cuddled together. David had his back to the doorway, but it was very clear that he was wrapped around his wife, holding her close.

Jade hesitated. She hadn't seen her sister in more than six months, and that had just been a brief visit. It had been tense and uncertain, and she'd left feeling even more wretched than the first time they'd argued over Kayla's choice of partners.

But where did sisterly concern end and unwanted meddling begin? Jade stepped away from the door and took a seat in the hallway. She'd once promised to try and understand Kayla's unusual relationship. If she upset Kayla now, would her sister push her out of her life completely? Would she refuse Jade's help when her relationship failed?

Making a decision she hoped she wouldn't regret, Jade left the hospital quickly. With a strange paranoid feeling of being followed, she slid into her car and headed for home.

* * * *

"I lost her," Mitchell said out loud as Zack pulled his car into the parking space beside him. His heart felt heavy, his gut hollow, like a part of him had been torn away. Zack quickly got out of the car and wrapped his arms around Mitchell.

"It's okay, babe," he said with a confidence he was far from feeling. "We'll find her."

"Zack, she was frightened of me. I caught a quick flash of memory, something in her past that scared her really badly, and somehow that fear transferred to me."

Zack nodded as he held his lover tighter. He'd also felt the woman's fear, had even understood it came from a memory and not Mitchell's actions, but he had no idea what it meant for their Taydelaan link. Even now he could feel the way the woman had felt in Mitchell's arms. In his mind he could feel her soft curves, smell her sweet scent. There was no doubt she was their third.

They just had to find her.

Chapter Two

Nearly three months later…

Jade woke from yet another erotic dream. She'd somehow expected that the dreams would stop while she visited her sister. Although, considering the fact that she'd packed her vibrator, even she hadn't really believed that.

Her nights were becoming increasingly disrupted by unfulfilled lust, and she was beginning to wonder if it was her brain trying to tell her that her biological clock was ticking. She pushed herself into a sitting position and ran a hand through her hair, trying to loosen the knots her thrashing about had caused.

She practically growled when she realized how badly her hand was shaking. At this rate she was never going to get any sleep. Her clit throbbed, her ass pulsed, her breasts ached, and if she closed her eyes she could still see her dream lovers. She tried to convince herself just to go back to sleep, but a full minute of tossing and turning convinced her it wasn't going to happen anytime soon.

After a moment of indecision, she finally reached into her suitcase and pulled out her battery operated boyfriend. She giggled a little nervously as she realized she'd probably used this toy more in the past three months than she had in the two years since she bought the damn thing. She stopped laughing when she saw the newest toy still in her suitcase—a beginner's butt plug. She'd never even considered anal play before, but since the dreams had started her imagination had gone completely wild. Hell, she'd even dreamed of being tied down and spanked.

Considering how frightened she was of being trapped and unable to escape, it had been very strange to enjoy such a dream. She wasn't even sure where the dreams of two men had come from. Somehow she'd woven a fantasy around the guy she'd run into at the hospital three months ago, but she couldn't explain how her overactive imagination had morphed that brief encounter into a blazing hot threesome.

She turned the vibrator on its lowest setting, sincerely hoping the noise wouldn't carry to the other occupants of the household. It was weird enough to be staying in her sister's home while her sister slept in bed with a married couple. The last thing she needed was to wake them with her nightly imaginary encounters.

Jade stroked the vibrator gently over her tingling nipples, and closed her eyes, her imagination picking up where her dream left off. Two men, the men from her dream, lay on either side of her. Each smoothed a hand over her stomach and up to her aching breasts. Gentle fingers plucked at her beaded nipples, and she sucked in a startled breath when they both pinched a nipple tight and then soothed the sting with their tongues.

Two heads, one dark, one light, dipped closer to her chest and laved the erect nubs soothingly. They each ran a hand over her abdomen and dipped lower, tangling in her curls before pressing against her mons. Gentle fingers stroked her slippery labia before pressing into her tight heat.

Trying not to lose herself in the fantasy, Jade lowered the vibrator to stroke it across her already swollen clit. Her legs shook as her orgasm beckoned, but she pulled the toy away, needing to prolong the sensation. She imagined the vibrator was a tongue rolling around her pussy, licking along her slit, dipping slowly inside her folds. She moaned as the feeling morphed, and she could almost feel hands holding her thighs wide, her lover thrusting his tongue deep into her core, another sucking hard on her breasts.

She pulled her knees up, pushing the toy into her pussy at the same time, fucking herself harder. She groaned as her dream lover moved over her and thrust hard into her body, claiming her, marking her, making her his own.

Harder and deeper he thrust into her, filling her, owning her, controlling her. She almost screamed as her orgasm shook through her, her legs shaking, her fingers going lax around the handle as her pussy grabbed at the small toy. The delicious sensations skittered over every inch of her body, her head falling back, her eyes closing as she savored the sensation.

She smiled sleepily as she felt whisper-soft kisses on her face as her dream lover withdrew from her with a contented sigh. But her eyes flew open as she felt her other dream lover slam into her. Confused to find herself still alone, Jade tried to deny the feeling of a long, thick cock fucking her hard and fast. She could feel her legs lifted high and wide even though physically she hadn't moved. She gasped as she felt her ass lifted off the mattress, her anus tingling as something hard pressed against her dark hole.

Orgasm slammed her, every muscle bucking, throbbing, jumping as liquid lava drenched her veins. She panted hard, trying to catch her breath, trying to quiet her low moan, even as the anus pulsed and the sensation of something hard being pushed into her continued.

Finally, gasping, sweating, exhausted, she fell back against her pillows and willed her breathing to return to normal. She closed her eyes as the actual sensation of the vibrator registered in her consciousness. Tiredly, she reached down and pulled the toy from her aching pussy. She barely had enough strength to turn the damn thing off before sleep claimed her.

* * * *

Mitchell woke from the dream just as hot cum pulsed onto his stomach. Holy hell, their woman was hot. He'd dreamed of her nearly every night since bumping into her in the hospital. He knew that she shared those dreams—and thanks to their mating link, so did Zack—but he wanted it to be real. Wanted to really touch and love and cherish their Taydelaan. If only they could find her.

Zack lay on his side, wide awake, looking down at Mitchell. "I think she woke up this time," he said with a huge smile on his face.

"Seriously?" It wasn't that Mitchell didn't believe his partner. It was just that the news seemed too good to be true. If their Taydelaan was able to retain her link to them even when she was awake, it meant that either their link was growing stronger, or maybe that she was physically closer to them. Hope rolled through his brain.

He glanced at the clock and realized that it was still very early. But as much as he wanted to roll over and go to sleep, the sticky evidence of his own orgasm stopped him. He grabbed the soiled sheet, wiped it over his chest, and then turned to Zack to do the same. His lover smiled indulgently as he touched Mitchell's face softly.

"I wouldn't mind a hot bath. What do you say, babe? Want to join me?"

Mitchell smiled and nodded his approval. They'd shared quite a few hot baths lately. Their midnight dalliances with their dream lover had often ended when their woman had woken up, leaving them both hard and aching for her. At least they'd had each other to slake their lust, but until tonight they'd worried that their Taydelaan had lain in her bed alone and unfulfilled.

Well she was alone—a fact he was selfishly grateful for—but at least she'd used her vibrator to find some relief.

As Zack went to fill the bath, Mitchell stripped the sheets from the bed and grabbed a clean set. He doubted that they'd get much more sleep today, but at least this gave them the option.

Zack was already running the bath by the time Mitchell joined him in the room. Even after such an incredible orgasm with their woman, the sight of his mate sitting naked on the edge of the tub as it filled with water, had his cock rising with interest. Zack smiled when he noticed the lust in Mitchell's thoughts.

"Is that for me?" Zack asked in a teasing tone. "Or are you still thinking of our Taydelaan?"

"Both," Mitchell answered honestly. He loved his mates equally, even if he'd never actually met their woman. Zack grabbed a folded towel and dropped it on the floor at Mitchell's feet. He knelt at the same time that he wrapped a warm fist around Mitchell's hard cock.

Zack licked at the bulbous head, running his tongue over and around the slit weeping pre-cum. He smiled up into his lover's eyes and then engulfed the full length, sucking hard and pumping the base with his fist. Mitchell groaned as memories flashed into his head of the incredible dream sex they'd just shared with their Taydelaan. Zack closed his eyes as he sent his own memories into Mitchell's mind, sharing with him the incredible sensations of fucking their woman.

Mitchell gaped as a thick digit found his ass and pressed inside. The sting intensified for a moment as Zack pressed his dry finger into Mitchell's anus. Somehow the feeling seemed more intense without lube, and Mitchell moaned when the finger slid over his prostate again and again and again. He held Zack's head carefully as he began to rock into his mouth in the same rhythm. His groin felt hot, his blood seeming to boil as the feeling intensified and rippled through his body. Zack hummed against his cock. Mitchell held his breath a moment, his eyes squeezed closed, trying to hold on to the sensation a moment longer.

But Zack twisted the finger in Mitchell's ass, and he lost control. Fucking his lover's face, harder, faster, thrusting deeper, holding him tighter, Mitchell erupted in his man's mouth and held him close as he swallowed. Lovingly, Zack cleaned Mitchell's cock with his tongue, rasping over the hypersensitive skin as Mitchell tried not to move.

"Bend over the vanity," Zack ordered as he pulled the finger from Mitchell's ass. Mitchell moved quickly to comply, always turned on when Zack took control like this. "Watch in the mirror."

Mitchell watched his lover in the mirror as he squirted lube onto his fingers and then pressed the cold liquid against Mitchell's anus. Zack's fingers slid in, scissoring against the tight muscle to loosen it. Mitchell pressed back against him, eager to feel his lover's cock, but Zack slapped his ass and ordered him to stay still.

Mitchell groaned as the sting morphed into heat and flowed down to his balls. Amazingly, his cock stirred to life, and he had a brief moment to wonder where his sudden stamina had come from before images of fucking their woman while his lover fucked him filled his mind. He could sense Zack's satisfaction as he weaved the fantasy for the both of them.

Finally, Zack fit his cock against Mitchell's hole and slid deep. They both groaned at the amazing sensation. Zack pulled out slowly, slamming back in quickly as if he couldn't bear not to be inside his lover. Again and again he pulled out and slammed back in. Mitchell braced himself against the vanity as he watched his lover plough his ass, and together they imagined him fucking their woman.

Sweating, panting, gasping for air, Mitchell tried to slow his heated rush to ecstasy to no avail. Cum splattered the vanity as Zack pushed into him one last time. He could feel his lover's dick throbbing as he poured himself into Mitchell's back passage. Mitchell wrapped an arm behind him, awkwardly holding his lover close.

The image of their Taydelaan coming beneath them took them both by surprise. She shook, she screamed, she writhed, and it was almost as if they could both see her, feel her, taste her.

Finally the image slid away, and once again it was just the two of them, intimately joined in their bathroom.

"We have to find her."

Mitchell gulped in air, trying to catch his breath as he nodded in agreement.

Chapter Three

Jade tried to hide the lingering feeling of being well loved. Hell, even after she'd gone back to sleep she'd somehow managed to have another dream and another orgasm. She even felt a little swollen from fabulous sex that she hadn't really experienced. The vibrator wasn't large enough nor did it vibrate strongly enough to cause this sort of lingering feeling. She literally felt well and truly fucked.

"Good morning," her sister said as Jade wandered sleepily into the kitchen.

"Morning," she mumbled, heading straight for the coffeepot. She grabbed a mug off the shelf above and filled it to the brim with steaming black nirvana. Hopefully the caffeine would wake her up and stop her from saying anything stupid.

"You okay?" her sister asked, her voice laced with a good deal of concern.

"Sure," Jade managed to force out in a cheerful tone. When Kayla narrowed her eyes in disbelief, Jade hoped she'd be satisfied with a half truth. "Just didn't sleep very well. Miss my own bed." Kayla nodded slowly like she doubted her sister's story, but fortunately she let the subject drop.

"Thank you for coming," Kayla said quietly, and for half a moment Jade's brain misinterpreted the meaning of her words. Coming? Yep, she'd done that all right. But then the actual meaning of Kayla's words finally registered, and Jade smiled softly.

"You're my baby sister," she said in a teasing tone. "Where else would I be?"

Kayla smiled and laid a hand over hers. "I know this hasn't been easy for you to understand, but they love me, and we all love our little girl, and well, it's wonderful that you can share this special day with us."

Jade nodded, trying desperately to hide her skepticism. "Our" little girl? Sometimes Kayla spoke as if she truly was the child's mother, and as her older sister, Jade often felt the need to correct her. But again she bit her tongue. Their relationship had been strained for a while now, and she missed the closeness they'd shared when they were younger. If accepting her sister's unusual relationship at face value was the cost to having Kayla back in her life, then that's the price she would pay.

"So what happens at this ceremony?" she asked, trying to sound interested instead of concerned.

"It's sort of like a christening in a way, but not really a religious thing. More of an introduction and naming ceremony in front of our friends and family."

"How many people are you expecting?"

"Not many," Kayla said as her eyes slid away from Jade. Her little sister had never been able to lie to her, and Jade snorted in disbelief.

"That many, huh?"

Kayla had the good sense to look embarrassed and then gave her a rough estimate. "About a hundred or so."

Considering that Jade was Kayla's only living family, that meant most of the guests were either friends or from Jessica and David's families. Jade was about to prod for more information when the baby monitor kicked in and a baby's high-pitched squeal broke through.

"Sorry," Kayla said, not looking sorry at all, "Jessica and David are out, so I need to go change her." Jade nodded her understanding and watched as her sister headed out the door. There was another advantage to a biological clock that was ticking toward the end—no dirty diapers. Jade had never been the clucky type, so it had been easy to convince herself that she was fine without ever becoming a mommy. Even sweet little Emily with her big blue eyes and chubby wrists hadn't swayed her from her conviction.

She finished her coffee slowly, making sure Kayla had plenty of time to change and dispose of any dirty diapers, and then wandered down the hallway to the nursery. Maybe she should've knocked, but considering it was only her and Kayla and the baby in the house, she felt fairly comfortable that she wouldn't walk in on anything she wasn't supposed to see. Oh boy, had she been wrong.

"What the hell are you doing?" she asked before she could censor her words. Kayla looked up, shock filling her features before she took a deep breath and spoke calmly.

"I'm feeding my daughter," she said without taking her eyes away from Jade's face. She stared at her, almost daring her to show her disapproval.

"Do Jessica and David know you're doing that?" Jade asked in disbelief. Until this moment she hadn't realized just how delusional her sister had become. But Kayla simply smiled, half laughed, and nodded. Still freaking out, Jade blurted another question. "H…how are you doing that?"

Kayla smiled warmly and said, "Same way other mothers do it."

"But you're not her mother. You didn't give birth to her."

Kayla looked down at the child nursing at her breast and then looked over to her sister with a sad smile. "She is my daughter. I know that's hard for you to believe, but it's the truth." She seemed thoughtful for a while and then looked at Jade apprehensively. "David and Jessica want me to explain it all to you." She smiled as if she'd thought of something funny and then continued. "Jessica and David just pulled up in the driveway. They want to be here as well. Apparently," she said with a smirk as if she were talking to someone else in the room, "I'm liable to leave out some important details."

* * * *

Hours later, Jade's mind still spun with worries. Her sister was obviously delusional and her partners were feeding her fantasy. Hell, judging by the turnout at the naming ceremony, she'd fallen into a cult of some kind. Many of the people present had appeared to be trios not couples. And if that wasn't weird enough, most of them had children also.

The fact that Kayla's fascination with science fiction was being exploited and encouraged by a group of equally delusional people just made the whole thing a lot harder to deal with. Fuck, Jade had read stories about cults like these, and none of them had been pleasant. Once they sucked someone into their beliefs, it was damn near deadly to pull them back out.

"Are you okay," David asked as he sat in the seat beside her.

"Peachy," she answered sarcastically. It probably wasn't wise to antagonize the man who thought he was an alien, but she couldn't seem to get her emotions under control. David reached over and took her hand in his own.

"It wasn't easy for Kayla to accept either, but we'll help you through it. Anything you want to know, you just need to ask." Great, the man was already trying to pull her into their delusional little world. Annoyance rose strong and bitter in her throat.

"Sure," she answered with a grin that probably looked more like an aggressive show of teeth, "where'd you park the spaceship?"

David laughed and smiled happily. "Kayla said you had sarcasm down to a fine art. I'm glad to say she didn't exaggerate." He laughed quietly to something only he understood and turned his smile back to her. "Kayla also says that if you'd just pull the carrot from your ass you'd be a lot more comfortable."

Jade didn't smile. That was something that Kayla had been telling her since the brat had grown old enough to sass her. There might only be five years between them, but their parents' deaths so long ago meant that Jade had been forced to grow up a lot faster than she would've liked. But Kayla had been barely thirteen, and someone needed to be responsible for her well-being.

"I know you care for her," she said to David, carefully trying to choose her words, "but surely you can see how unfair it is to let her believe that Emily is her daughter."

David looked slightly exasperated but smiled regardless. "I know you don't want to believe, but we are telling you the truth. Emily really is the child of three parents, just like many of the others here." Jade glanced around the room filled with strangers milling about. Everywhere she looked people stood laughing, socializing, enjoying the party. Only Jade seemed to be the odd one out. "How about," David said, obviously not thrilled with the idea, "you suspend your disbelief for one night and enjoy your time with Kayla. I know how much she misses having you in her life."

Tears prickled at the back of her eyes. She'd missed Kayla so much over the last few years that the job that she loved and the home that she'd decorated exactly to her own tastes had both started to feel stale, boring, lonely. More than once she'd considered throwing it all away and following her sister to this less than major metropolis. But following her sister like a lost puppy had simply felt wrong, so she'd dragged herself through her day-to-day life and somewhat convinced herself she was happy.

She nodded to David, and he smiled and wrapped an arm around her shoulders. "Come on," he said softly. "I know Kayla wants our daughter to bond with her Aunt Jade." Jade nodded and tried to be happy even as her head screamed at her not to fall headfirst into Kayla's delusions.

Chapter Four

"She's here!" Zack said as soon as he stepped out of the car. His Taydelaan's essence niggled at his senses. Mitchell nodded his agreement as they both clambered out of the car and headed into the reception area. If they hadn't wasted all day searching the city for the one woman who could complete them, they would've found her hours ago. How lucky were they to find their Taydelaan at a Sesturian Naming Ceremony?

Hope and anticipation were quickly replaced with disbelief as they entered the main room and found their woman in the arms of another man. Zack's temper flared white hot, and the woman stiffened and looked over her shoulder. He knew the exact moment she recognized him, because her eyes widened, her heartbeat sped up, and her panties dampened. Good, at least he wasn't going to have to beat the crap out of the man with his arm around her.

The man beside her dropped his arm and turned to see what Mitchell and Zack's Taydelaan saw. Zack finally recognized his old friend and breathed a sigh of relief that David was happily married. It didn't explain why he had his hands on Zack and Mitchell's woman, but it was a convenient way to finally learn her name.

"David," he said through clenched teeth. He could feel the same tension coming off Mitchell. Goddess help David if he was stupid enough to get in their way. "Care to introduce us to your friend?" David looked startled at first but quickly brightened when he glanced at the woman beside him.

"She's the one?" he asked, pointing his thumb at the woman with a wide grin plastered on his face.

"Yup," Mitchell growled.

"Zack, Mitchell, I'd like to introduce you to my sister-in-law, Jade."

That stopped Zack for a moment. Sister-in-law? Was their Taydelaan Sesturian? But then the other possibility entered his head and he breathed a sigh. The genetic scientists had assured them that their Taydelaan was a human female, that's why they'd spent the last five Earth years on this backward planet searching for her.

"Kayla's sister?" Mitchell asked in a rough voice. Zack could feel his lover's nervous energy. He wanted, no needed, to claim the woman in front of them. Shit, Zack could even feel the enzyme starting to produce in Mitchell's body. If he'd ever doubted Jade was the one, it was well and truly settled now.

"That's right," his woman said as she crossed her arms and gave him an aggressive look. He grinned at her attitude. His woman was fire and ice, and he was going to love every moment of their time together.

He could feel Mitchell's caveman instincts roaring to the surface, but it was the niggles of fear coming off Jade that had him moving to calm his lover. He slid his arm around Mitchell and held him tight against his body, his hand running soothingly up and down his partner's side.

"It's lovely to finally meet you," Zack said as he held his hand out for Jade to take. She looked at his outstretched arm but didn't move to touch him.

"Finally?" she asked with an eyebrow raised to telegraph her skepticism.

"You mean, you don't recognize the men from your dreams?" He grinned triumphantly as her eyes widened, but then she pulled the reaction back under control, glanced over her shoulder, nodded as if she'd been communicating with someone, and turned back to them.

"It was nice to meet you," she said dismissively and turned to leave. Mitchell practically growled beside him, and Zack gave a pleading look to David. After three months of sharing dreams with the woman, he already felt like she belonged with them, and to watch her walk away like this was sending his thought processes into chaos. His confusion was nothing compared to the instincts driving Mitchell.

They'd both heard stories of forced matings. They hadn't quite believed the wild descriptions about the enzyme, but considering the nearly out-of-control urges they were both feeling, the legends had to be true. Hell, at this rate one or both of them was going to do something truly stupid, like throwing the woman over their shoulder and dragging her back to their home.

David was studying Mitchell closely, and he cast a worried glance to Zack before Kayla joined their little group. She wrapped her arm through Jade's, effectively holding her in the conversation. Mitchell seemed to calm a little now that their Taydelaan wasn't about to walk away, but he was still on edge, still struggling for control.

"Why don't the five of us find somewhere more private to talk?"

"Private?" Jade squawked, looking terrified.

"Jade," Kayla said, calling her sister's attention, "Zack and Mitchell traveled a long way to find you. The least you can do is give them a few minutes to explain."

"Traveled?" Jade asked, sounding confused. But then it was like a lightbulb switching on. Her eyes narrowed, her jaw firmed, her lips drew into a thin line. Zack struggled to hold his lover back. The type of challenge their Taydelaan was throwing at them was the exact opposite of what Mitchell needed right now.

"Get her out of here," Zack whispered urgently, hoping, praying that David heard him clearly enough. He must've relayed the information to Kayla because she quickly turned her sister around and practically dragged her from the room. Jade looked confused and terrified and everything in between, but Zack could only concentrate on one lover at a time. Mitchell needed him. Needed to mate with his lover. Now that the enzyme was producing, his instincts were taking over, and he could no longer think clearly.

Zack very nearly had to carry Mitchell into a side room. He nodded a quick acknowledgement when he saw David take up a protective stance in front of the door. Zack turned to lock the door and found himself pressed hard against the wood, his lover's cock jammed between his ass cheeks, their clothes the only thing separating them.

"Need to fuck you," Mitchell growled brokenly as he scraped his fangs over Zack's neck and shoulder. Zack nodded, trying to soothe his lover with their telepathic connection. Shaking hands wrapped around him, cursing the belt buckle, the snap, and the zipper on his dress pants. Zack tried to help him, worried that Mitchell might resort to ripping the damn things just to get them off.

He managed to snag the small tube of lube from his pocket before Mitchell pushed the offending material to the ground. Thank the goddess that they'd been lovers for years. If this had been their first time together, the rough claiming might've shocked him. He managed to slick lube onto his hand and grab his lover's cock for the briefest of moments before the hard rod rammed into his back passage.

He nearly howled at the rough entry but could barely breathe as his lover pulled him far enough away from the door to bend him over and thrust deeper. Over and again, slam in, pull back, slam in again. A tight fist wrapped around Zack's cock, and he panted heavily as his lover reamed his ass. Trapped in his lover's suddenly superior strength, Zack grunted, trying to hold himself against the door, hoping it was solid enough to handle their incredible fucking.

And it was incredible. He'd never been taken this thoroughly before. He felt possessed and surrounded and owned but also completely and thoroughly loved. "Love you," Mitchell managed to breathe just a moment before his fangs sank into Zack's neck and pumped the enzyme into his blood.

Mitchell's movements turned explosive, and Zack moaned his release even as Mitchell held his cock tight, refusing to let him blow. Again Mitchell's speed increased, but Zack's knees gave out and he half collapsed against the door. With strength likely linked to the enzyme's production, Mitchell held him up, dragging Zack back onto his cock again and again.

Mitchell finally withdrew his fangs as his own orgasm started. He grunted and held Zack hard against him. Zack moaned just before unconsciousness claimed him.

* * * *

Mitchell collapsed to his knees, remorse and fear for his lover warring with the relief that they'd finally mated properly. He pulled his cock gently from Zack's ass, relieved to see that there wasn't any blood. Zack looked red and sore and swollen, but at least Mitchell hadn't caused any serious injury. Thank the goddess his lover had retained the foresight to get some lube onto his cock. Mitchell knew without a doubt that he would've taken his lover without it if none had been available. He shuddered at the implications. Zack had loved him and protected him since the moment they met. Mitchell hated the idea that he would've let his man down if he'd been given the chance.

He shuddered as he lowered himself to the floor and pulled his lover into his arms, cradling him protectively as he tried to wake him. Fear nearly choked him before Zack opened his eyes, but when he did it was to smile seductively and pull Mitchell's head down for a slow, lingering kiss.

"Love you," he said as he caressed the side of Mitchell's face. Tears of relief filmed Mitchell's vision, but he refused to let them fall. Zack closed his eyes tiredly and slumped back against Mitchell's chest. *"Next time,"* he whispered into Mitchell's mind, *"we'll find somewhere more comfortable."*

* * * *

"What the hell?" Jade grouched as her sister drove the car like a maniac. "First you want me to talk to them, and then you drag me out of there like the place is on fire."

Kayla didn't seem to be listening, and Jade growled in frustration. The woman was probably having one of her delusional, fictitious conversations with her so-called partners. Jade had always considered her younger sister quite intelligent, so how the hell had she let herself imagine voices in her head?

"Do you have any idea how delusional you are?" she yelled at her sister.

"Do you have any idea how much trouble you caused back there?" Kayla countered.

"Trouble? What the hell did I do?" She shook her head, trying to clear the strange emotions flying through her brain. She was completely pissed at her sister, so why the hell were her nipples tingling? She crossed and uncrossed her legs as heat swam through her veins and lust curled low in her belly. What the fuck?

Kayla finally slowed the car to reasonable speeds and took a moment to smirk at her sister.

"That's them you can feel."

"Them who? And what the hell do you know about what I'm feeling?" She was tired of this bullshit. None of it was real. Fuck, somebody probably dropped a date rape drug into her drink. "Take me to the hospital," she demanded as she suddenly felt the walls closing in on her. She gulped in a great lungful of air, trying to calm the rising panic. Usually she got this feeling from being trapped in an elevator or pressed into a crowd of people, not just sitting in a car.

"Kayla," she practically begged. "Please take me to a hospital. I think I've been drugged."

Kayla glanced at her in concern, but instead of turning the car back toward the hospital, she pulled off the highway and stopped on a side street.

"Jade, listen to me," she said in a kind and calm voice. "You need to trust me, okay?" Jade managed to nod her head. She did trust her sister, despite her current circumstances and circle of friends. "You haven't been drugged. What you're feeling is the mating heat."

"The what?" Jade yelled, feeling like she wanted to crawl out of her skin. "Enough of the space aliens bullshit, Kayla."

"Those two men back there," she said quietly as if Jade hadn't just yelled at her, "are your Sesturian mates. You are their Taydelaan. You're the one who completes their triad."

"Fuck off," she yelled, trying to understand how she could yell at her sister and still feel the urge to grab her vibrator. "If I'm their mate then how come you pulled me away? If I'm so fucking special to them—" She gasped as orgasm rolled through her. Shit, even with her sister beside her she couldn't squash the incredible sensations. She moaned low in the back of her throat as her pussy convulsed, fisting against nothing.

Jade closed her eyes as complete mortification rose to bite her in the ass. She really didn't want an explanation for that. She was pretty sure there wasn't a drug capable of making a woman orgasm without some type of physical stimulation as well.

She laid her head back against the seat and silently prayed for her sanity. First the dreams with delicious strangers, then the actual face-to-face meeting with said strangers, and now an orgasm in the middle of nowhere with no stimulation—could things get any weirder? Maybe she was the delusional one and Kayla was actually sane.

"Don't cry," Kayla said quietly. "It's not as bad as it seems. The mating link is quite pleasant once you get used to it." Jade wiped at her face, surprised to find she actually was crying.

"I don't understand any of this," she said on a breathless whisper. "Why is this happening to me?"

"Simple," Kayla answered with a shrug. "You're a Taydelaan, and there are two Sesturian males who will spend the rest of their lives proving it to you."

Chapter Five

Zack woke as a soft knock sounded through the solid wood door. Thank the goddess for solid wood. It would've been quite embarrassing if Mitchell's rough claiming had managed to push Zack through the door and into the party area. Hell, the way Mitchell had been under the enzyme's influence it wouldn't have been enough to stop him.

"Come in," Zack called when it seemed Mitchell wouldn't, or couldn't, talk. Zack glanced down at the last moment, remembering his state of undress, but was grateful to realize that Mitchell had managed to pull most of his clothes back into place. He looked ragged and thoroughly fucked, but at least he didn't have his ass hanging out.

David poked his head around the door without opening it all the way. "Everything okay?" he asked with a concerned frown.

"Of course," Zack said, still sitting in Mitchell's lap. "Everything's under control now."

David nodded and stepped into the small room, closing the door firmly behind him. He held something out and offered it to Mitchell. "Take it," he said. "It'll help suppress the enzyme for a short while."

Mitchell reached up to take the small rod, and Zack could sense his intense relief and gratitude. "Is Jade okay?" He looked really worried, and Zack stroked his hand down his lover's stomach, trying to soothe the man physically as he whispered mental reassurances that everything would be okay.

"She's confused and angry and really, really embarrassed but otherwise fine."

"Embarrassed?" Zack asked, not really understanding why Jade would feel embarrassment. It's not like Zack or Mitchell had gotten close enough to say or do anything.

"Yes, embarrassed that she just had an orgasm in the car five miles away." David laughed at the shock on their faces but then turned somber once more. "You're already linked to her, aren't you?" When they both nodded, he asked the inevitable question, "How?"

"She bumped into me at the hospital the day Emily was born, but she left before I could stop her. We've been dreaming about her ever since. Usually when she wakes up that's the end of it, but last night it felt like she was closer, like even when she did wake up the three of us were still connected." Zack felt Mitchell nod against the top of his head, confirming his explanation. "We traveled all over town trying to find her—"

"Which explains why you missed Emily's naming ceremony," David said with a quirked eyebrow.

"Yeah, sorry about that," Zack said, apologizing for the timing rather than the actual nonattendance. "Anyway, as soon as we pulled into the parking lot, we felt her. By the time we got into the room, Mitchell was already producing the enzyme, and, well, you were there for the rest."

David nodded, seeming to choose his words carefully. "Kayla is trying to explain everything to Jade as we speak. We've already told her most of it, but she doesn't believe anything. The words 'delusional,' 'cult,' and 'ridiculous bullshit' have made quite a few appearances in our conversations."

"I need to see her," Mitchell said, sounding completely miserable.

David nodded. "I know, and I understand. When I couldn't claim Kayla, I almost went insane. Hell, if Jed hadn't been able to supply me with some of the suppressant, we might've lost Kayla before we could determine if she was truly our Taydelaan."

Zack knew the story. Jessica, Kayla, and David's mating had been just as unusual as Mitchell, Jade, and Zack's was turning out to be.

Goddess, if only things had gone the way they were supposed to, Mitchell wouldn't be producing the enzyme yet, Zack wouldn't be worrying for both his lovers, and Jade wouldn't be scared half out of her mind.

"It'll work out," David said sincerely. Zack felt Mitchell's rise in hope, but David quickly burst the bubble by suggesting they go home without their Taydelaan. "Just for tonight," he assured them.

Mitchell surprised him by nodding in agreement, and then he helped Zack to his feet and climbed back onto his own. "We'll explain it all to her," David said confidently, "and hopefully we'll be able to set something up tomorrow night."

Zack grabbed his lover's hand and squeezed reassuringly.

"And if that doesn't work?" Mitchell asked anxiously.

"Then you can always visit her in your dreams."

David winked and left them to tidy up.

* * * *

Jade paced back and forth. They'd traveled the rest of the way back to the house in silence. Jade could still feel the lethargy from her embarrassing orgasm. But of course her baby sister was still trying to convince her that everything was okay.

"No, no, no, this doesn't make any fucking sense, and I refuse to listen to any more of your bullshit." This was ridiculous. How many times did she have to tell Kayla she wasn't buying the shit she was shoveling? Kayla looked upset by her attitude, and Jade was too tired to care. If Kayla didn't want to have this conversation all she had to do was walk away. Her sister looked angry enough to spit, but she suddenly calmed and a slow smile spread across her face.

"Fine. Whatever," she dismissed with a flip of her hand. "Ignore me. It's been a long day. Why don't you just go and get some sleep?"

Sleep? Oh, that was such a lousy idea. Sleep was what started this whole mess in the first place. Sleep wasn't going to help her, not by a long shot. Her sister's smirk told her everything she needed. "You know," Jade accused in a tight voice.

"Know what?" Kayla asked in that innocent-sounding voice she'd tried to use since the day she'd been old enough to lie.

"You know about the dreams."

"Now, how could I know about the dreams," she said lightly. "According to you I'm delusional and not actually hearing my partners' thoughts in my head. Isn't that right?"

"No, I mean yes. I mean, what the fuck do you want from me?"

Kayla looked upset at her expletive. Well that was just too damn bad. Jade might've refrained from using swear words around her baby sister while she was filling the role of substitute parent, but according to Kayla, she was a parent now herself, so tiptoeing around her younger sister was no longer necessary. And quite frankly, Jade was just a little too freaked out to care about a swear word or two.

"Jade," Kayla said with a sympathetic smile, "I just want you to be happy. Zack and Mitchell are great guys, and if you just take a chance you'll learn that for yourself."

"Okay," Jade said tiredly as she turned toward the room she'd been using. "I'll try, but I can't promise anything. This is all just a little too freaky to take in all at once."

"I know how you feel. The day I saw the matter transporter dissolve a dozen boxes in the living room really freaked me out, too." She smiled fondly at the memory. "But I gave it a chance and I've never been happier. I want that for you, too. You deserve to be happy, Jade. Just let it happen."

Kayla reached over, pressed a kiss to Jade's cheek, and whispered softly, "Pleasant dreams."

* * * *

Mitchell was too agitated to do anything needing more thought than pacing back and forth required. He'd spent the last half hour rubbing soothing lotions all over Zack. Hell, the enzyme had given him far more strength than he'd thought possible and he could've hurt both his mates badly. Thank the goddess that Kayla and David and Zack had been able to protect Jade from him. When she'd challenged him with that sassy stance, he'd nearly lost it. Every primitive emotion had risen to the surface, and he'd only been able to think in single words—dominate, subdue, possess.

He shuddered again as he imagined how frightened Jade would've been if he'd been able to follow through on his baser instincts. He swallowed painfully. What if he'd done to her what he'd done to Zack? Heat burst through his abdomen at the thought, and his cock roared to life once more. Damn.

"Babe," Zack said from his position on the bed, "come here."

Mitchell went to him gladly, relieved to hear his lover's command. He'd always assumed that being the more confident, more dominating of the two of them, that Zack would automatically be the partner to produce the enzyme. Feeling it build in his own body the moment he'd seen Jade had been quite frightening, the explosive effects terrifying.

"Don't," Zack said, again obviously hearing the fears in Mitchell's head. "You did nothing wrong. And you didn't hurt me." Mitchell closed his eyes again, still having difficulty believing his lover's reassurances. A firm hand lifted his chin, and Mitchell opened his eyes to stare in his partner's beloved face. "I quite enjoyed it actually." When Mitchell huffed in disbelief, Zack smiled and said, "Maybe not the part where you almost smooshed me through a door, but I loved how much you needed me, how much you wanted me, and I've never felt more loved. Look into my heart," he said reassuringly, "see the answers for yourself."

Mitchell did just that. He'd refrained from looking too closely at his lover's emotions since their lovemaking—if you could call that rough claiming making love—terrified of what he might find hidden in the depths of Zack's emotions. But when he finally opened his heart and his mind to his lover, all he saw was nothing but love and deep respect. He closed his eyes in relief.

"Thank you," he said sincerely, trying to let Zack understand every emotion he owned.

Zack pulled him closer. "I love you, babe. No matter what happens with our Taydelaan, we'll always have each other. I promise you. Any time you need some relief from the enzyme, I will be here for you."

Mitchell nodded his head and curled into his lover's embrace, more than a little relieved to be held this way. "I need you," Zack whispered, echoing Mitchell's earlier words.

* * * *

Jade woke as she moaned in her sleep. Confused and disoriented, she moaned again as a featherlight touch whispered over her skin. Was this really happening? Or was she still sleeping? She didn't even know what to believe anymore.

"Please," she whispered quietly to the empty room. "What do you want from me?"

"We just want to love you, Jade," a voice said inside her head. She somehow knew it belonged to Zack even though she'd barely exchanged more than a few words with the man. *"Are you in bed?"* She nodded her head in reply, but somehow he understood her, and she felt something akin to a wolfish grin tickle her mind. *"What are you wearing?"*

Surprised, she laughed out loud at the lecherous question. Fortunately the voice laughed with her, and Jade sighed when she got the feeling that he'd made her laugh on purpose. She managed to relax just a little. "I'm sorry about before," she said sincerely. "I didn't mean to upset you."

"Oh, beautiful," another voice said—she could tell this one was Mitchell—*"I'm sorry I scared you. Did Kayla explain about the enzyme?"*

"She said it starts producing when you make a strong link with your Taydelaan. Is that what I am to you?"

"Yes," they answered in unison.

"Why?" she asked. This is the part Kayla couldn't or wouldn't explain. "How do you go about picking your Taydelaan?"

"We don't get to choose," the voice said seriously. *"A Taydelaan is determined by nature or genetics or the goddess. All we know is that there is one perfect match for us and you're that one."*

"So it's not me you want, it's my genes?"

"We want in your jeans, yes," Zack joked, deliberately ignoring her question. How she knew it was deliberate she wasn't sure, but she could tell that her question had hit a sore point.

"So how does this work? We meet, we fuck, we produce a baby, then what?"

She could feel disapproval at her flippant question, and a small part of her wanted to take it back, but she was being driven by emotions even she didn't understand now.

"Then we live happily ever after," Zack said just as flippantly. She could sense his determination to trivialize the matter simply by making it all sound like a corny fairy tale. But this wasn't a fairy tale, it was her life, and if she was going to buy into this nonsense, she wanted to know how she—as the baby-carrying third—fit into the grand scheme of things. It was obvious that they loved each other deeply. She didn't think she could live on the fringes of their love, collecting the scraps whenever they came her way.

"Oh, for fuck's sake, woman, you will drive a man insane. If I was there, I'd flip you over and tan that perky ass. Taydelaan just means the third partner to be found. It has nothing to do with rank or order or anything else. We will love you exactly the same way we love each other."

"But you don't even know me," she said, trying to hide how much the idea of Zack spanking her ass really turned her on.

"Don't bother trying to hide that thought," Mitchell said in her head. *"Remember that dream where we tied you down and spanked you to orgasm? We already know that you loved it."* She flushed hot and cold at the memory. She'd woken covered in sweat and would've sworn her ass was bright red if the mirror hadn't told her otherwise.

"So you know I have a kinky side, so what? That doesn't amount to love."

"Baby, if I hadn't promised your brother-in-law that we'd give you time, we'd be on your doorstep in five minutes quite happily showing you how much we do know about you."

"That's just sex," she said, feeling wretched inside. "You know nothing about the real me."

"Beautiful, if you don't give us a chance to prove our love," Mitchell said in a voice filled with hope, *"how will you ever know if you're right?"*

"Have dinner with us tomorrow," Zack added. *"We'll pick you up, spend some time getting to know each other, and if you're not convinced, we'll bring you back to your sister's place. All you'll have to do is tell us. We won't stop you from leaving, but we're asking you to give us a chance."*

"What about the enzyme?" she asked nervously. "Will that happen again?"

"No, beautiful, I have a way to suppress it for a short time so that we can get to know each other without the pressure to mate." Jade sensed his intense relief that he'd be able to control it. She even understood that it was a proven medicine and not some home remedy. *"Please, Jade, just give the three of us a chance."*

"Okay," she whispered, hoping she wouldn't regret it.

Chapter Six

Mitchell frowned at the lopsided flower arrangement and scowled at the burned first course. He'd wanted everything to be perfect, but somehow that hadn't happened. He couldn't wait to get back to Sesturia. The primitive way of cooking on this planet had been the bane of his existence for three years.

"Relax," Zack told him as he came into the room. "Jade will appreciate that you tried. It doesn't need to be perfect."

"How do you know that?" he asked, unconsciously revealing insecurities he'd tried to keep hidden. "Is your link to her stronger than mine?"

Zack looked shocked by the question and took a moment to look deeper into Mitchell's mind. He frowned when he came across what Mitchell had been trying to keep from him. "I should whip your ass for even thinking that." Mitchell's cock twitched at the threat, and he tried to hide a smile by coughing into his hand. Zack grinned and stalked over to stand in front of Mitchell. "No, my link is not stronger. I just know Kayla. Jade took care of her when their parents died. She couldn't have raised someone as sweet as Kayla without being a special person herself."

Mitchell nodded in agreement. He should've thought of that, but he was just feeling so stressed he wasn't thinking very clearly. The fleeting thought of what Zack usually did to help him relax whispered through his mind, but he quickly squashed the impulse.

Zack pouted, but he smiled when he realized Mitchell's reason—Jade would sense what they were up to. "Maybe she could use a little stress relief, too." He winked but didn't push. "Do you know she's as nervous as you are?"

"She is?" Mitchell asked, surprised that he'd missed that. He'd probably sensed it but dismissed it as an echo of his own stress. He longed for the day when all three of them had a full mate link. Maybe that's why he was so nervous about tonight. This was the beginning of the rest of their lives, and he couldn't afford to fuck it up.

Zack hugged him once more and moved toward the kitchen to remove the casserole that Mitchell currently seemed to be burning. Damn.

* * * *

Jade glanced at her brother-in-law and tried not to be obvious when she ran her sweaty palms down her jeans. Mitchell and Zack hadn't been impressed that she'd asked David to drop her off instead of letting them come for her. She hadn't meant to be cantankerous, but things had seemed so far out of her control, she'd argued on the one point she felt she could win. It didn't help that she was more nervous about this single date than she'd been with every other date put together. Why was she so damn jumpy?

"You can probably sense Mitchell's stress, baby," Zack whispered in her head. *"He's more nervous than I've ever seen him. Be gentle with him."*

She smiled at Zack's teasing words but somehow understood the seriousness behind them.

"The link has gotten stronger," David said with a nod of approval. She glanced over at her sister's husband and tried to smile. She didn't quite manage it, but he glanced over and smiled for her. "I've known Mitchell and Zack for years. They're good guys."

"So everybody says," she answered, trying not to be sarcastic. Other than some really hot sex dreams she knew very little about them. The fact that she could hear them in her head and feel their emotions several miles away did nothing to convince her that she wasn't insane. "How long have you known them?"

David looked a little uncomfortable and gave her an answer that didn't really satisfy. "Many, many years."

"How many years?" She couldn't quite shake the feeling that David was hiding something.

He breathed out heavily and finally gave her a proper answer. "About forty Earth years."

"What? Did you really say forty years? You're joking, right? You don't look a day over thirty, how can you have known them for forty years?" She could feel hysteria creeping over her. This couldn't be right. How could this be right? "How old are you?" she demanded, practically holding her breath as she waited for his answer.

"Seventy-four," he said, sounding resigned and maybe a little annoyed that he'd started this conversation. "And before you go asking, Jessica is a few years younger."

"Baby," Zack said with a singsong voice inside her head, *"tell David I'm going to kick his ass when he gets here."* She couldn't help but grin at the threat delivered in such a sweet voice. David glanced over, looking at her worriedly.

"Zack says he's not happy with you." She delivered the message while trying to ignore the fact that she was essentially relaying a conversation with a voice in her head. David grinned, and a soft laugh escaped him.

"I reckon he probably wants to kick my ass," he said, confirming that he knew the man well. "I'm sorry, Jade. I didn't mean to start this conversation, but as a general rule, Sesturians have a life expectancy about twice that of humans."

"So I'll be old and gray while Zack and Mitchell still look young?" Despite all the jokes she'd made about maybe one day trying her hand at being a cougar, she really didn't like the idea of looking twice the age of her partners. She felt a swell of hope in her mind and realized it came from Mitchell and Zack. Was she really thinking long term with these two?

"Not quite," David said slowly, and she got the impression that he was once again trying to avoid answering. "Sesturian medicine is quite advanced, but I'm sure that's something you and your partners can discuss at a later date." She nodded, willing to let David off the hook, for now at least. "We're here," he said, sounding very relieved. "I have very strict instructions from Kayla to walk you to the door, threaten bodily harm to Mitchell and Zack if they fail to treat you properly, and then get my ass home."

Jade tried to hide the smile threatening to break free but failed miserably. She could just imagine her sister giving those exact instructions. David smiled with her and whispered conspiratorially, "Just be glad she's not in your head, too." He grinned, obviously listening to Jade's younger sister give him grief via telepathy.

"Thank you," she said sincerely. David was a genuinely nice guy, and even though she hadn't been happy when Kayla had begun her relationship with David and Jessica, it was obvious that they both loved her sister as much as they loved each other.

"Call me when you want to come home," David said with a grin and a wink.

* * * *

Mitchell could feel her affection for David, and it was driving him nuts. He knew—absolutely knew—that it was just the emotions a woman would have for any member of her family, but a primitive part of him wanted to keep her all to himself.

"It's okay," Zack said in a soothing telepathic voice. *"It's just the effect of the enzyme. Once you've claimed her, things will go back to normal."*

"What if she never lets me claim her?" he asked out loud in a sullen voice. He was starting to understand the strange mood swings pregnant woman went through. This whiny, negative, insecure feeling was pissing him off, but he couldn't seem to shake it.

"She will," Zack said confidently as he went to answer the door.

"Hello, baby," Zack said as he reached for Jade's hand, "welcome to our home."

The overwhelming urge to haul his woman over his shoulder and lock her in his bedroom for several days slid through Mitchell's mind, but he managed to control it for the moment. The suppressant David had given him was helping to stop the enzyme's production but didn't seem to do anything to control his possessive urges. He took a deep breath, trying to calm himself before he did something stupid. He glanced at Zack for reassurance and realized that the possessive urges had been there all along. It was just his fear that Jade would reject them that was magnifying everything.

"Hello, Zack." She let Zack pull her into his arms for a brief hug, and Mitchell felt his cock roar to life. Seeing both his partners together was a far bigger turn-on than he'd ever imagined. He wanted to grab them both, love them, protect them, and fuck them both until none of them could walk straight. Zack and Jade must've picked up on that thought because they both moved into the circle of his arms and held on tight. The feeling of finally being complete washed through him, and he held them both for a long time.

"Yup," David said as he stepped out the front door, "that's my cue to leave. Take care of her." Mitchell nodded his promise and relaxed even more when Jade stretched up onto her toes and pressed a soft kiss to the underside of his jaw.

* * * *

Zack had no idea how long they stood like that in the hallway, but eventually the smell of burning food reached his nostrils. He was tempted to simply ignore it, but figured burning down the house was probably not the best way to take care of their girl.

"How do you feel about pizza?" Mitchell looked startled by the question, but then the smell of burning food reached him as well. He pulled Zack and Jade closer for a brief moment and finally released them. A deep rumble of a laugh escaped his chest.

"So much for perfect," he said, sounding calmer than he had all day.

Jade must've noticed the smell, too, because she smiled and nodded. "Pizza sounds great. Extra anchovies for me."

"Ugh," Zack said with a shudder. "You better kiss me now, baby, because once you've downed a few of those salty little things you're going to need a bucket of mouthwash before I kiss you again."

She looked startled at first but then realized that he was joking—well, maybe half joking. He really, *really* hated anchovies. Jade followed them into the kitchen, and Zack turned everything off, refusing to think of the cleanup they'd need to do tomorrow. Goddess, he missed the food processors on Sesturia. Perfectly cooked, nutritionally balanced, quickly delivered meals with very little cleanup. What could be more perfect?

"Good to know about the anchovies," Jade said with a grin. "If I ever need a break from your kisses I know exactly what to do."

"Doesn't work with me," Mitchell teased. "I'm fine with anchovies."

She smiled at them both, but it faltered and she suddenly looked very lost. Her knees wobbled, and he went to steady her, but she held her hand up for him to stay where he was. She grabbed one of the chairs at the breakfast bench and sat heavily.

"I'm sorry," she said tiredly. "I don't even know you. I've never actually kissed you, so I don't understand why I said that."

"Beautiful," Mitchell said as he stepped closer. He touched her cheek affectionately. "You do know us. You can already sense our emotions. You already hear our thoughts. The link is already there, and it will only get stronger."

She looked from Mitchell to Zack and back again before she tried to say something. She had to swallow before she could voice her thoughts.

"I…I never expected to…to find someone. I thought I was just one of those people who was meant to be alone. I don't understand how I could be your Taydelaan."

"Do you want to be alone the rest of your life?" Zack asked as he tried to understand the myriad of emotions he could feel flowing through her. She shook her head, and he felt relief pour through both him and Mitchell.

"Then kiss me, beautiful," Mitchell said, taking the seat beside her. "Kiss me and let the link grow. Then you'll understand you belong with us."

Her eyes were filmed with tears when she looked at Mitchell, but she leaned over and pressed a gentle kiss to his mouth. Zack could feel Mitchell's determination to let her control the kiss, and he watched, fascinated, as their Taydelaan kissed his lover for the first time. Her tongue touched Mitchell's lips, and he groaned and stroked it with his own. Jade lifted off the chair and moved to sit on Mitchell's lap as she deepened the kiss and raised the heat in the room.

With his hand rubbing gently over his own erection, Zack watched Jade turn to straddle Mitchell's lap, pressing her crotch against his hard cock. Mitchell groaned and lifted her onto the kitchen table. He kissed her frantically, taking control of the kiss, stamping her with his possessiveness. She writhed against him, and Zack almost came in his jeans when Mitchell grabbed Jade's shirt and ripped it from her body.

She gasped, the sound loud in the otherwise silent kitchen, but didn't pull away. Mitchell dragged her bra away just as roughly, and Zack stepped closer to help with her jeans. He was more than willing to keep their woman naked for the rest of her life, but they might need her jeans if they planned to walk out the front door.

He managed to undo the material and wiggle them down her hips. Mitchell lifted her off the table, and Zack dragged the material down her legs and off her feet, taking her shoes with them. Mitchell placed her back in the middle of the table, finally breaking the kiss and moving away from her slightly.

She lay on the table like an offering from the gods. Zach could barely breathe as he moved to the side and lowered his head to kiss her. She wrapped her arms around him and welcomed his tongue into her mouth, sucking gently as he explored the dark recess. He felt Mitchell's deep satisfaction that they were kissing this way a moment before he lowered his head to Jade's pussy. Zack could feel her pleasure course through her as his lover lapped at her hidden folds.

Zack moved a hand to pluck at one of her beaded nipples, smiling when she arched her back and lifted from the table. Through the connection with his mates, he could feel Jade's surprise that she liked what Mitchell was doing, and Mitchell's relief that she was enjoying it. Zack felt the exact moment that Mitchell stiffened his tongue and started fucking her with it. She shivered and pulled Zack closer as her orgasm spiraled nearer.

Fucking her mouth with his own tongue, Zack matched Mitchell's rhythm and held their woman down, knowing from their dreams how much the immobility turned her on. He felt a moment of fear pass through her before her orgasm exploded. She moaned as every muscle shook with her release. Mitchell held her thighs open, prolonging her climax with the clever use of his tongue. Over and over she undulated against the hard table, her muscles rippling, her breathing labored, her heart and mind open to them both.

Zack thought he sensed something about a man from her past, but that part of the link dissolved before he could understand it fully. Mitchell leaned over the table, turned Zack's head with a firm hand, and thrust his tongue into Zack's mouth. Jade's taste burst on his tongue, and he moaned at the perfection of the moment. Even in their dreams it hadn't been this intense. He could feel Jade's arousal winding higher again as she watched them kiss above her.

"Bedroom," Mitchell said in a tone that suggested he wouldn't take no for an answer. He smiled and watched Mitchell lift their woman into his arms. Zack followed them into the bedroom, almost surprised to realize that both he and Mitchell were still fully clothed. Jade lay in the middle of the bed, watching them shyly as Zack moved to undress his lover. He wanted to watch the two people most important to him connect in the most elemental of ways.

Mitchell grinned at the thoughts he so obviously sensed, pulled him closer, and ravaged his mouth in a kiss that left his knees wobbly. Zack fought to catch his breath as Mitchell undid his own jeans, kicked them off, and then turned his attention to Zack. He barely had the jeans to his knees before Mitchell took Zack's cock in his mouth. Zack groaned at the delicious and familiar sensation as his lover sucked hard against the head while swirling his tongue over the thick veins. Mitchell engulfed him and swallowed, dragging his cock deeper still. He could feel Jade's excitement as she watched.

Just knowing that the woman who completed them liked what she saw was almost enough to have him coming down his lover's throat. But Mitchell chuckled and slowly slid his mouth away from Zack's cock. "Do you want a taste, beautiful?" he asked Jade as he held a hand out to her. She nodded enthusiastically and quickly climbed off the bed to kneel at Zack's feet.

She wrapped a soft hand around the base of his cock and licked the end with her tongue. Over and over she laved him like ice cream. His eyes nearly rolled into the back of his head when she sucked him into her warm mouth. Mitchell knelt behind her, his hands roaming all over her, his groin pressed hard against her ass cheeks.

"Can you swallow him, beautiful," Mitchell asked out loud in a rough voice.

She nodded against Zack's cock and his excitement ramped much, much higher. Mitchell's large hands grabbed his ass, pulling him tighter against Jade, forcing his cock deeper into her mouth. She fought his hold for a moment, but Mitchell whispered instructions and she breathed through her nose and swallowed around Zack's cock.

"Good girl," Zack managed to say even though he could barely breathe. He felt her happiness a moment before Mitchell pushed a couple of lubed fingers deep into his ass. Panting at the incredible twin sensations, Zack's eyes did roll into the back of his head as Jade sucked harder, pumping the base of his cock rhythmically with her hand, matching perfectly the plunge and withdrawal of Mitchell's fingers in his ass.

Practically lifting onto his toes, heat boiled in his groin, as his cock grew even harder. He nearly vibrated on the spot as his lovers pushed his arousal into the stratosphere. No longer in control, Zack flexed his ass muscles, grinding deeper, thrusting harder as he burst in Jade's mouth. He held her head to him as she swallowed and then suckled gently as his cock softened in her mouth.

Mitchell tapped him on the ass as he stood. "Back in a minute," he said as he headed for the bathroom. Zack watched his lover walk away then bent and lifted Jade off her knees and helped her back onto the bed. She snuggled into him, and he held her tight, loving the feel of her soft curves against him.

Zack heard water running for a brief moment and then sensed Mitchell giving himself an extra dose of the enzyme suppressant. He smiled at the protectiveness he could feel. Mitchell wasn't willing to force the enzyme onto Jade until she was willing to accept them both. Despite knowing that the enzyme would bind her to them for the rest of their lives—thereby shortcutting the necessity to woo their woman—Mitchell was determined that she come to them by her choice.

Zack couldn't have loved the man more than he did at that moment.

Mitchell came back into the room with a happy smile on his face. He knelt at the edge of the bed, touched Jade's face with his large hand, and whispered the question they both wanted answered. "Can we make love to you, beautiful?"

"Yes," Jade answered immediately, her gaze flicking between them both. "I would like that very much." Mitchell climbed onto the bed and lay on his back beside her.

"Come here, beautiful." Zack helped her to straddle Mitchell, holding the man's cock steady so she could lower herself onto his hard length. All three of them groaned as she impaled herself slowly. She stopped for a moment, and Zack could sense her letting her body adjust to Mitchell's thick cock. He realized with a jolt of surprise that it had been a long time for her since she'd had anything wider than her slim vibrator inside her body. Feeling ridiculously possessive, he ran his hands over her back and ass as she finally slid Mitchell's full length inside.

She went to move, but Mitchell wrapped his arms around her and held her still. Zack could sense the man's feelings of finally being complete and shared them. Finally having their Taydelaan in their arms was absolutely amazing, but it was the woman herself that made it so special. Even just the brief glimpses he'd had of her inner thoughts proved without a doubt that she was just as beautiful on the inside as she was on the outside.

Zack slid his hand down her spine, over her gorgeous, perfect ass, and dipped lower to caress Mitchell's balls. Mitchell lifted his hips off the bed, pushing into her harder as he held her hips tight against him. She moaned, and Zack could feel her arousal gathering, building higher, winding tighter. She cried out as Mitchell lifted her off his cock, and moaned when he lowered her back down. Over and over Mitchell controlled her movements, fucking her as he held her tight.

Zack caressed her labia, feeling Mitchell's cock slide in and out of the slippery flesh. He groaned when he found her clit swollen and begging for attention. "Yes," she hissed as he squeezed the tiny bud. He teased her, sliding his fingers over and around the engorged flesh as Mitchell moved her harder, faster, more urgently.

She screamed when her release began, and he flicked her clit over and over as he felt Mitchell swell and burst, pumping his seed deep into Jade's body, marking her as his own. Mitchell closed his arms around her as she collapsed forward onto his chest, trapping Zack's hand between them. She giggled softly as he managed to extricate his arm, but she held her breath when he pressed his fingers against her anus.

"Have you ever had a man in your ass?" he whispered as he swirled his slippery digits around the puckered entrance.

She had to gulp air twice before she could answer with a shake of her head. He gently pushed the tip of one finger past the tight ring of muscle, and he smiled gratefully as Mitchell held her still and caressed her spine soothingly. "You'll love it," Mitchell promised as she relaxed against his chest and let Zack push his finger deeper. A fleeting image of the butt plug she'd bought recently flashed in his head, and he smiled. Their girl had certainly thought about it.

"Top drawer of my dresser," Mitchell said with a smile on his face. Curious, Zack slid his finger from Jade's ass, groaned almost in unison with their girl, and headed for the drawer. He nearly whooped with delight when he saw the contents. How the hell had Mitchell managed to buy beginner's butt plugs without Zack noticing?

He grabbed a new plug and hurried into the bathroom to wash it. He covered it with a generous amount of lube and headed back into the bedroom. Disappointment rose momentarily when he thought she was asleep, but then he realized that Mitchell was whispering instructions in her mind, helping her relax, promising to take things slowly.

As Zack approached the bed, Mitchell carefully hooked his hands under Jade's knees and pulled them up the bed, opening her ass cheeks wider. Zack climbed onto the mattress, wedging himself between Mitchell's legs and caressing the most beautiful ass he'd ever seen. He touched the soft plug to her back entrance. Jade stiffened momentarily, so he waited for her to adjust to the new sensation before pushing the tip into her anus. Mitchell continued to reassure her through their telepathic link as Zack used steady pressure to push the plug all the way into her ass.

The widest part finally slid past the tight ring of muscle, and then he watched her muscles close around the thinner part, trapping the plug in her body. Goddess, the woman was perfect.

Chapter Seven

Jade sensed both men's deep satisfaction. She hadn't planned on falling into bed with them tonight, but something about it seemed so darn right. She moved slightly, and the muscles in her ass squeezed around the plug, sending heat blossoming outward. She gasped as the incredible sensation spun her arousal higher.

"Please," she begged.

"My pleasure," Zack whispered as he positioned himself behind her. He rubbed the head of his cock against her folds, and she felt a moment of fear. But Mitchell was there, holding her, soothing her, silently assuring her that she would enjoy being fucked this way. She relaxed, trusting them both.

Zack slowly worked his cock into her swollen pussy, gently sliding in and out until she thought she would go mad with her need for more. Zack lifted her partially onto her knees, and Mitchell slid his hand to her clit. As he swirled his fingers over the tight bundle of nerves, Zack finally increased his pace. He held her hips steady as he began to plunge deeper, breathe harder, fuck her faster.

She tried to push back against him, but he held her trapped, and she felt her arousal spin higher at the immobility. Images of the dreams she'd shared with them played in her head, and she practically screeched when her orgasm finally flowed through her. Pinpoints of color exploded behind her eyelids, every muscle shaking, every breath labored, every nerve ending finally satisfied.

She felt Zack's cock throb, pumping his seed deep inside her, marking her as theirs. Exhausted and well loved, she lay contentedly against Mitchell as he played with her hair and whispered how much he loved her.

****

Zack felt her spike in fear a millisecond before she sat up quickly.

"You love me?" she asked, her voice filled with shock, her eyes seeking Zack's. Mitchell eased her back down to his chest, pressing her face against his heart.

"Of course we love you," Zack said as he lay on his side and swept the hair from her eyes. "You can feel the mating link growing between the three of us." She shook her head in denial, but he could sense her deliberate attempt to lie. "Lying to me will earn you a spanking, baby." Zack nearly lost it when her eyes darkened with desire and she moaned softly, but he could still feel her intense fear.

"Jade," Mitchell said seriously, "we don't just love you because you're our Taydelaan. We love you for being a beautiful person, too. We love you because we can see into your heart and your mind and know who you really are, not just who you pretend to be." She blushed prettily but nodded her head in understanding.

"Then you know how confused I feel," she said quietly.

"Yes," Zack agreed, "but we can also feel how much you love us already. Jade, that will only grow as the link gets stronger. Eventually we'll know everything about each other. Every thought, every feeling, every memory."

Her complete panic caught them both by surprise, and she clambered off the bed before either of them thought to stop her. Her eyes filled with tears, her hands shaking, she shook her head in denial. "That's not what I want," she said, practically tearing Zack's heart from his chest. "I don't want you in my head twenty-four-seven. I want my own life, my own identity. I want to choose my own future, not go along with some predestined fate bullshit."

* * * *

Afterward she couldn't quite explain how she'd managed it, but somehow she pulled on her clothes, called her sister for a lift, and waited silently for her to arrive. She'd felt the intense hurt from both men but refused to let it in, denying their link the only way she knew how—by ignoring it.

She'd made it back to Kayla's home before she'd remembered the plug in her ass. Once she'd removed it, she'd had every intention of discarding the stupid thing, but something held her back. She washed it, wrapped it, and packed it in her bags, all the while steadfastly refusing to answer her lovers' telepathic pleas.

And within four hours she was home in her own bed—tired, miserable, and more alone than she could ever remember.

* * * *

Zack held his lover in his arms, trying to come to terms with their loss. Jade had not only left the area, she'd somehow managed to block their connection in their dreams. It'd been the longest week in both their lives, and Zack was seriously considering taking his lover home to Sesturia for a while. At least there they would have the love and support of their families.

He sighed as he tried not to think of the woman who'd invaded his heart. She'd been frightened the first time she'd met Mitchell in the hospital, and neither of them had been able to learn why. Zack had set the problem aside, arrogantly assuming that once the mating link became stronger that they'd know. But it seemed that by not pressing the point or asking her directly, they'd missed an important problem. He felt certain that whatever caused her sudden, nearly violent withdrawal was also the cause of her fear.

"I'm sorry," Mitchell whispered for the hundredth time. He was blaming himself, worried that he hadn't controlled the enzyme well enough, that he'd somehow scared their woman away. The link had been broken so completely that the enzyme wasn't even producing in Mitchell's body anymore. Nothing highlighted their loss more than that.

Zack heard the knock on the door and really wanted to ignore their unwanted visitor, but a moment later the bell rang several times, and it pissed him off enough to get his ass out of bed. He kissed Mitchell's cheek as he pulled the blankets back into place and then went to deal with their unwelcome guest.

But when he opened the door to Jed, his anger slid away, and he invited the official leader of the Sesturian community on Earth into their home.

Jed didn't waste any time with small talk. "I heard about your problems with Kayla's sister, and I wanted to make sure that you understood the situation."

Understood the situation? What was to understand? Jade didn't want them. End of story.

Jed watched him closely for a moment, as if he was reading Zack's body language, or maybe waiting for him to say something. Zack kept his mouth closed and his expression neutral. Jed may be the equivalent of a governor in his world, but he really didn't have a clue what Zack and Mitchell were going through.

"The concept of a Taydelaan is probably more complex than many of our people know. Your potential third isn't just one person, but rather a type of person," Jed began, managing to shock Zack into stunned silence in the process. Everything he knew pointed to a one and only Taydelaan, not a choice. "It's a combination of things that makes a Taydelaan a perfect match, but there is always more than one person who would fit the description. It's not a high number. It's something like one in half a million, but with six billion people on this planet, it means that there is a good chance that you will meet another woman who'll be your Taydelaan."

"But we want Jade," Mitchell said from the doorway. He leaned against the door jamb, looking tired and beaten, but he held his jaw stubbornly.

"Jade has already closed her connection to you," Jed said in the type of voice Zack had heard on self-help commercials—kind but firm. "If she wanted to be your Taydelaan, she wouldn't have been able to do that."

Zack could feel Mitchell's determination falter. She *had* been able to shut them out. It certainly wasn't the actions of a woman willing to love them. "What if she's just scared?" Zack asked, trying to deny how desperate he must sound. "What if something in her past made it difficult for her to accept our love?"

Jed considered his words for a moment and nodded slowly. "I suppose that could be true. Fear can override some pretty strong emotions, especially if memories intrude. Did you sense anything in the partial link that you had? Any memory or trauma that could explain her sudden withdrawal?"

Zack shook his head in frustration, but Mitchell pushed himself off the wall and stood taller. "The day I met her," he said, frowning as he tried to put into words what he'd felt, "she nearly freaked out when I tried to stop her walking away. I didn't do anything that could be considered threatening, but her reaction was well out of proportion. She practically ran the length of the hallway when I let her past."

"And after her…uhm…orgasm," Zack added, glancing at Jed in mild embarrassment to be discussing something so private with a man who was virtually a stranger, "I sensed something about an ex-boyfriend or ex-lover, something that left her feeling unloved."

Mitchell walked into the room and wrapped his arms around Zack. "I felt that, too," he said quietly.

"Well, I think the best thing you can do is go after her," Jed said decisively. "Find out what she really feels. If she truly doesn't love you, at least you'll know for certain and can move on with your lives."

And if she does love you, well I guess I'll see you at the Joining Ceremony." Jed shook both their hands and left without any fanfare.

"Let's pack some clothes," Zack said, already mentally planning their trip. Technically, Jade was only three hours away, so they could make the trip there and back in a day, but he had every intention of parking themselves on her doorstep until she admitted the truth or kicked them to the curb. Either way, he wasn't planning on it being a short visit.

* * * *

Jade pulled her car into the driveway and rested her head on the steering wheel, trying to find the energy to climb out of the car and into bed. Since leaving her men behind, she hadn't felt the inclination to do anything. She only went to work because she couldn't afford to lose her job, otherwise she would've stayed in bed for the entire week.

She caught movement out of the corner of her eye and looked over just as the door was flung open. Jade gasped as a rough hand grabbed her arm and tried to pull her from the car. The seat belt jammed, and a male voice cursed before leaning over her and undoing the clasp. Strong arms dragged her from the car and slammed her back against the door panel.

"Where the hell have you been?" The familiar voice made her cringe, and she really, really wished she hadn't come home today.

"Duncan," she said in a breathless, frightened voice even though she was trying to hide her fear, "why are you here?"

"I need more money," he growled as he kicked the car door closed and dragged her to the front door of her home. "And I don't like waiting."

She frantically searched through her bag, trying to find her keys with shaking hands. She knew from bitter experience that when he was like this the slightest thing could set him off. She swallowed nervously as her fingers finally wrapped around the house keys. She tried to fit the key into the lock, but he grabbed them from her, undid the lock, and pushed her inside ahead of him. For a crazy moment she considered shoving the door closed in his face, but she knew he'd quickly find a way in and his resulting anger would bring far more danger.

"Money," he reminded her as she stood dumbly in the hallway, wondering how the hell she'd ever considered herself in love with this man.

"I don't have much at the moment," she said truthfully. Hell, she could barely keep up with the day-to-day bills lately, and thanks to this man, her savings were nonexistent.

"Well then," he said, taking a menacing step closer, "this visit is not going to go well for you, is it."

"Duncan," she said, trying to sound reasonable instead of scared to death, "I gave you everything I had last time. I can't give you what I don't have."

"Fine," he said, sounding really pissed off, "I'll take your mother's jewelry." The only thing of any real value in her mother's jewelry box was her engagement ring, and she'd fight tooth and nail before she handed it over to this asshole.

"It's never going to stop, is it?" she asked, finally realizing that he would always be back for more. After the last time, she'd thought it was over, that he'd finally taken everything of value and would never be back. Obviously, she'd been wrong.

He laughed at her, his golden good looks and bright smile belying the beast within. "Well that depends, darlin'," he drawled as he stalked closer, "on how quickly you can get them pretty jewels for me. I might stop if you ask really, really nice like."

The look he gave her had her heart hammering in her throat. She could barely breathe. Panic wrapped her gut, squeezed tight. She knew what came next.

Chapter Eight

As Mitchell slowed the car so they could find the correct house, Jade's fear slammed into them like a sledgehammer. Momentarily stunned by the link's reconnection, Mitchell stopped in the middle of the street and glanced over his shoulder at a small, tidy house. He was certain that's where Jade was, but he couldn't identify the source of her terror.

He put the car in reverse and backed up to park the car out front of Jade's home. A quick glance at the letterbox confirmed the house number Kayla had given them. As he stepped out of the car he felt Jade's sudden spike in terror. She wasn't frightened of them. She wasn't even aware they were here. Something, or someone, inside the house was the reason for her fear. Terrified for her, he didn't bother knocking. Just burst through the front door.

Mitchell dragged the man away from her, his fist landing on the man's jaw before he could even consider the implications. Zack moved to help Jade. She still had her jeans on, but her shirt had been ripped in two.

The man groaned, pushed himself to his feet, and growled in irritation. "Who the fuck are you?" he yelled. "Get the fuck out of my house."

Mitchell turned to Jade, trying to understand what the hell was going on. Kayla had said this was Jade's house, that she lived alone. Mitchell saw the man's swift attack just in time to counter it. Off balance, Jade's attacker fell awkwardly into the wall.

"Your house?" Mitchell asked as he stood over the man aggressively. "Explain to me how this is your house."

"Simple, that whore," he said, pointing to Jade, "is my wife, so this is my house. Now get the fuck out of my house."

"Jade?" Zack asked the woman in his arms. "You married this asshole?"

"Divorced him, too," she said defiantly.

"Oh, look how brave you are now," the man said as he pushed himself upright and took a step closer. Zack moved to stand between Jade and her ex-husband. The man smiled mockingly at Zack's protective stance. "Don't worry, slut, when they get tired of your constant nagging, I'll be back to finish what I started." He laughed as he stepped out the door. Mitchell wanted to follow him out and finish what he'd started with his fists. But Jade's fear still called to him, and he moved to wrap her and Zack in his arms.

"I'm sorry," she said as reaction set in and tears started to fall. "I'm sorry that I hurt you. Th...thank you for coming to help me."

* * * *

Jade couldn't seem to stop the tears. She'd never felt more alone than she had when Duncan had been tearing at her clothes. If Zack and Mitchell hadn't chosen that moment to come through the door, she had no doubt that her ex would've followed through on his threats. He'd done so before. She shuddered at the filthy feeling the man's touch had left behind.

"I need a shower," she managed to sob through the unstoppable tears.

"Baby," Zack said as he held her carefully, "you should report this to the police first. You're already bruising around your breasts and stomach."

She glanced down at her chest, almost surprised to see the circular, finger-shaped bruises. Adrenaline still pumped through her veins and seemed to be masking the pain.

"I don't want to involve the police," she said as embarrassment slid through her. She should've reported him the first time he raped her, but she'd always felt particularly ashamed that she'd invited that man into her life in the first place. Explaining her stupidity to officers of the law just seemed too humiliating. Duncan had been threatening and demanding money from her for years, and that just wasn't something she wanted to explain in minute detail.

Mitchell nodded as if he'd heard every thought in her head.

"We'll protect you," he said in a strong voice, "but what happens to the next woman he chooses to harass?" Guilt warred with embarrassment even though she knew going to the police was the right thing to do.

"All right," she said, trying to swallow her misgivings, "I'll report him to the police. I never should've married the asshole in the first place."

"Why did you?" Mitchell asked.

"I don't remember," she said honestly. "I was tired of being alone, could hear my biological clock ticking, and wanted a family. I guess I didn't see the man for what he really was until it was too late." She shook her head, disgusted at her own weakness. Had she been so desperate for a family of her own that she'd considered Duncan suitable father material? "It only lasted four months," she said softly. "I didn't even tell Kayla. But you're right. I need to report him to the police. I should've done it a long time ago. I just wish I could do it without looking like the worst type of fool."

"Maybe you could," Zack said with a mischievous grin. "Derek does owe me a favor."

"True," Mitchell agreed.

"Who's Derek?" she asked as a small hope unfurled in her belly. Dealing with Duncan without feeling completely humiliated would be a good solution.

"Derek is the Emnurian scientist in charge of human studies."

"Emnurian?" she repeated, feeling completely lost by Zack's supposed explanation.

"Sorry, baby," he said as he led her over to the sofa and pulled her down beside him. "Emnurian is the name of the alien species behind most of the reported abductions. They usually put the test subjects back unharmed, but I'm sure Derek can leave enough fear in your ex's memory to put him off trying to intimidate anyone. Derek could probably do a complete personality overhaul if he tried."

"Would that stop Duncan from harassing me or another woman silly enough to fall for his lies?"

"Absolutely," Mitchell said from the kitchen. She nodded her agreement but was sidetracked by his next question. "Where are your tea bags?"

"Tea bags?" Okay, that was getting to be an annoying habit. She had to stop repeating everything they said. Sheesh, any minute they were going to wrap her in cotton wool and hide her from the world.

"Is that what you want?" Zack asked in a strained voice. "To be coddled and sheltered?"

"Not really," she said, finally realizing that the mate link was open and stronger than ever. "It probably sounds really selfish, but I want to make my own decisions, be responsible for my own choices, and choose the course of my own life, but at the same time I want someone I know I can lean on if things get too tough."

She felt their surprised reactions but couldn't seem to understand them.

"Baby, what you want is exactly what we're offering." She looked from Mitchell to Zack and back again, and then closed her eyes as she tried to find words to explain exactly how what she wanted differed from what they offered.

"You don't understand. I had no *me* when I was married to Duncan. Everything I did was measured by his needs and wants, not by my choice, not ever," she said, wishing she could just fall into their arms and pretend that everything would be all right. "I need to be my own person. Sharing a mating link like the one you describe robs me of that."

"How?" Mitchell said as he came closer, the tea bags obviously forgotten.

"It just does." God, she was lame. Why couldn't she explain how having them in her head all the time would take away her freedom to make her own choices? How the very thought of being left to the whims and manipulations of another person again scared her more than being alone? Why couldn't she just tell them she needed to be a whole person, not just one part of a group of three?

"Is that how you really see the mating link?" Zack said, sounding slightly amused.

Anger curled in her belly at the feeling that he was somehow laughing at her. He growled and kissed her, thrusting his tongue into her mouth and the memories of what they'd shared into her head. "Baby," he said when they finally came up for air, "the link only enhances our relationship. None of us will ever lose the part of us that makes us individuals. Does your sister seem any different since joining with David and Jessica?"

She shook her head. No, if anything, Kayla was more herself now than she was when she'd been dating that asshole who'd hurt her years ago.

"You know us," Mitchell said as he sat on the sofa and pulled Jade's hand into his own. "You know our personalities. You know what's in our hearts. Why would you ever think we'd want you to not be the woman we fell in love with?"

"But I'm your Taydelaan. You didn't choose me."

"Now see that's where you're wrong," Zack said, sounding rather cocky once more. "For every couple, there is more than one Taydelaan. Granted they are few and far between, but—"

She cut him off. "How few and far between, exactly?" she asked suspiciously.

"About one in half a million," Mitchell filled in.

"But," Zack said, looking exasperated by both of them, "the point is that of the twelve thousand possible matches on this planet, we chose you."

"You chose me?" she asked, even knowing that she still sounded like a parrot but this time not caring.

"Do you think that if we hadn't chosen you that the link would've continued to grow? What if you'd been married, or too young or...I don't know...too nasty...do you think we would have been able to share the dreams we did?"

"I almost am too nasty," she said, feeling guilty for the way she'd treated them. She'd reacted out of fear to a situation she didn't fully understand.

"No," Zack said as he tilted her face up to his with his fingers, "too wary perhaps, but never nasty. Even when you left us, we knew it was because something was frightening you, driving you away, not you deliberately being nasty."

"I love you," she whispered. She felt both of them relax as if they'd been holding their breath, waiting for her to demand her freedom once more. "I'm sorry I hurt you," she said, knowing even as she said the words that she was forgiven. She smiled as she felt the mate link solidify even further in her mind.

"We love you, too," they said in unison.

Epilogue

"I can't believe I let Kayla talk me into that," Jade complained as she fell into the closest armchair. "I would've preferred a small reception, not that massive party." She grumbled out loud, but both of her partners could feel her satisfaction that the ceremony had gone off without a hitch.

She still wore her wedding dress, and Mitchell couldn't imagine anything more appropriate. The soft, flowing material accented her shapely beauty and highlighted her natural coloring. She looked absolutely perfect in it.

But that didn't mean he wasn't dying to get it off her.

Mitchell smiled as Zack sensed his growing arousal, and then moved to lift their wife into his arms. Together the three of them had decided to spend their honeymoon at home and were eagerly planning to visit Sesturia on the next transport. Zack and Mitchell's parents were already organizing another Joining Ceremony for when they arrived home. Mitchell just hoped that Jade didn't find the experience too overwhelming. Fortunately Kayla, Jessica, and David had chosen to travel back to Sesturia at the same time, so Jade had her sister to turn to if she needed.

"You look beautiful in this dress," Mitchell said. "But you need to take it off before I accidentally damage it." She laughed softly as he sent images to both Jade and Zack of what would happen if she didn't hurry.

"But first," Zack said, "I promised you a wedding present."

"That you did," she said as Zack placed her on her feet and lifted the dress over her head. She wore a soft silk bra and matching panties.

Zack turned to sit on the end of the bed and slowly lowered their wife facedown over his lap. Mitchell felt his cock twitch and his blood pressure rise as he realized the present Zack intended to give them all.

Mitchell loved the feel of Zack's hand on his ass, but being able to watch both his lovers while feeling their reactions was almost enough to have him coming on the spot. Jade went willingly, trusting her mates to give her pleasure. Mitchell dragged his clothes off, desperate to release his cock from the tight confines of his pants. He could already feel the enzyme starting to build, and this time he would let it. Tonight he'd make them a true triad.

* * * *

Jade moaned as Zack caressed her ass through the silk panties. She'd been anticipating this night for days now, knowing that Mitchell would finally inject her with the enzyme. She shivered at the full implications and stories her sister had shared. Being claimed by your mate was supposed to be the most erotic of experiences and she'd waited with a mixture of nervousness and longing. She almost felt like a virgin bride.

But the gift that Zack was offering was just as special. She'd never actually been spanked before. The dream they'd shared had been exciting, but she'd wondered what it would feel like to be spanked for real. It looked like she was about to find out.

Jade relaxed as the first blow landed, the impact softened by the thin material of her panties, and smiled as Mitchell stepped closer. "Take them off," he growled at Zack. Zack caressed her ass as Mitchell roughly dragged the scrap of material down her legs. Zack pressed her head down further, pushing her off balance, making her feel more vulnerable. Mitchell undid her bra and let it fall to the ground.

The second blow was a lot harder, and she felt tears prickle the back of her eyes as the third hit lower on her thigh. Again and again, over and over, Zack's large hand heated her bottom. She bit her lip, wondering why they couldn't feel her discomfort, but then something amazing happened. Heat swelled outward, inflaming her clit, heightening her desire. She started rocking into the blows, needing them, anticipating them, begging for the next one. Her world narrowed to this small room, her two men, her coming orgasm. She barely breathed as her climax swelled through her muscles, her body undulating against Zack's lap, her eyes squeezing closed as she shook violently.

Rough fingers pressed into her pussy, filling her, fucking her as her muscles pulsed against them. Zack adjusted her slightly, and Mitchell lifted her head to run his cock against her lips. She opened for him, gagging slightly as he thrust deeply. She managed to swallow but cried out when another hand found her clit and squeezed hard. Her orgasm rolled back through her as the fingers fucked her in time with Mitchell's thrusts. Mitchell pushed into her over and over, holding her face, giving her no reprieve. His frantic movements faltered, his orgasm taking him by surprise.

* * * *

Zack watched the man and woman he loved have the most incredible orgasms he'd ever seen. He felt everything they felt, heard everything they thought, and practically came with them. Only the thought of what would happen after Mitchell bit her with the enzyme stopped him from losing it right then and there.

She shook as her orgasm slowly ebbed, sucking lovingly on Mitchell's spent cock. She made a sound of disappointment as Mitchell finally pulled out of her mouth. He leaned over and caressed her face, smoothing the tears away from her eyes, watching her closely as they both used their telepathy to check she was all right. She smiled at Mitchell, assuring them both through their mate link that the tears weren't important.

"I love you," Zack said to them both as he helped Jade to her feet. She clung to him, her legs wobbly, but she gave him the most brilliant smile. She must've seen the thoughts that flitted through his mind because she answered the one question he'd been too frightened to ask.

"Yes," she said with a huge grin. Mitchell pressed up against her spine, pushing her into Zack's embrace.

"Are you sure, beautiful? We have plenty of time to start a family."

"Hello?" she said, sounding really confused. "I'm in my mid-thirties. If we don't start now, we're liable to miss our chance." She was only thirty-two and he didn't consider that mid-anything, but it seemed clear that she didn't really know the full extent of the enzyme's effects. That was the trouble with the mate link. Before it was complete, the information that came through was kind of like Swiss cheese, full of holes and incomplete.

"Baby," Zack said as he pulled her closer, "the enzyme changes you a little, and makes you not quite human, but not quite Sesturian either. Once Mitchell injects you with it, you'll only be able to have children with us, no one else."

"I know that," she said. She pressed a soft kiss to the underside of his jaw. "And I know that I need both of you to come inside me within a minute or two of each other, or even," she added with a nervous swallow, "come inside me at the same time." Zack smiled at the image she described. It brought a whole new meaning to the words "double penetration," and he could barely wait to try it. But he wanted Jade to know they had options and didn't need to start a family straight away.

"But what you don't know," Mitchell said with a soft laugh, "is that the enzyme extends your life expectancy…and your reproductive years."

"Really?" she asked, sounding quite pleased. "You mean I won't be old and gray, while you two still look in your thirties?" Zack smiled and pulled both his lovers closer.

"No, baby," he said as she wriggled against him to get even closer, "we'll grow old and gray with you."

She was quiet for a moment, and the three of them stood together, simply enjoying the closeness. "I would still like to start a family tonight," she said quietly, "but if you want to wait—"

Zack stopped her words with a smack on her thigh. "Tonight is a perfect time to start our family," he said as he caressed the smooth skin. "Climb on the bed, baby. We're going to help you relax."

Mitchell helped her onto the bed, arranging her on her back, pushing her legs wide as Zack positioned himself between her thighs and pressed a kiss to her mons. He could smell her sweet scent, and only the promise of what was to come kept him from slamming his cock into her wet heat and fucking her until neither of them could walk.

She moaned, obviously picking up on his internal thoughts. Even without the enzyme their mate link was growing rapidly. He dipped his tongue into her pussy, pressing her thighs harder against the bed as she writhed against his mouth. Gently he explored her folds, pressing deeper, tasting the cream of her last orgasm.

"You taste delicious," Mitchell said even before he leaned over and pressed his mouth to Zack's. She lowered her hands, trying to hold them to her, trying to lift her pussy and fuck their faces, but Mitchell moved to gather her wrists and pin them to the bed.

* * * *

Mitchell watched as Zack pleasured their woman, tormenting and teasing her pussy and clit until she was begging for release. But each time she neared the pinnacle, Zack moved away, slowing things down, heightening the anticipation.

The enzyme was building rapidly, and Mitchell wondered how much longer he could control the darker, more elemental impulse to claim his mates. He could feel both Jade and Zack inside his head, soothing him, encouraging him, calling to him. Jade stiffened a moment before orgasm claimed her, every nerve ending vibrating with her release.

Unable to control the enzyme's effects any longer, Mitchell leaned over her, trapping her against the bed, and his fangs lowered and he bit into her neck. The enzyme pumped into her blood, and she screeched as a second, more powerful orgasm slammed through her. Mitchell could feel his cock, hard and aching, leaking pre-cum as Zack lifted off the bed and hurriedly removed his clothes.

With his last scrap of sanity, Mitchell rolled onto his back, dragging Jade with him. She straddled him, quickly lowering onto his erection, sighing like she'd finally found where she belonged. He held her close, amazed to realize just how solid their mating link was now. Even his link with Zack had grown stronger.

Mitchell grinned as he sensed Zack climb onto the bed behind them and then drop a kiss on Jade's pinkened ass. She moaned at the reminder of her first spanking, and Zack promised them both in a sensual telepathic voice that it wouldn't be her last.

Zack pushed their legs open, kneeling between them, his hands roaming over the place where Mitchell and Jade were joined.

* * * *

Jade felt no fear. Even though she'd never done this before, even though the very idea made her worry how they would fit, she knew that her men would keep her safe regardless. No matter how turned on they felt, or even how harshly the enzyme affected Mitchell's thought processes, their first instincts had always been to protect her.

She could feel their love. Actually feel it growing as the link strengthened. She could see their memories, feel their emotions, understand their motivations, and she knew—absolutely knew without a doubt—that they would love her for the rest of her life.

The enzyme still coursed through her, but she could easily discern her thoughts and feelings from Zack and Mitchell's emotions. She felt part of a triad but still herself. She was still the person she'd always been, but now she was loved and cherished and completely whole.

She gasped as Zack slipped his fingers into her pussy, caressing her inner walls and Mitchell's cock at the same time. Jade breathed out, trying to relax her muscles so that Zack could stretch her vaginal walls and she could take them both.

Jade giggled nervously as she felt Zack spread lube on his cock. She could feel his determination not to hurt her, and she loved him even more. Mitchell moved, pulling his cock out of her slightly, and she could feel Zack's cock rubbing against his, sliding together as they placed both heads against her slit and pushed in slightly. She moaned as her muscles embraced them, pressing their cocks together as they slid further into her body. Both men shook trying to slow their build to orgasm, but their possession felt so amazing that she found herself rocking against them, trying to hurry their pace.

Zack grasped her hips, pushing her harder against Mitchell, her swollen clit pressed between them, the intense sting and amazing heat spreading over her entire body. They thrust deeper, stretching her, possessing her, loving her. She lifted her ass, straining to take them both, begging with her body.

Orgasm slammed her, her pussy, her ass pulsing, throbbing, dragging them closer. She screamed as she felt them lose control, felt them press harder, deeper, faster. Each movement exquisite agony as they thrust into her together. She felt Mitchell's fangs, the brief sting, the heat of the enzyme, and her world exploded into a million bright colors and shiny stars. She felt them both swell and pour their seed deep into her body. Their whispered reassurances and loving caresses making her feel more complete than she'd ever felt at any time in her life.

"I love you," she whispered to them both, squeezing her inner muscles as they slowly slipped from her body. "When will we know if we've made a baby?" Even as the words came out of her mouth she realized she already knew the answer. This mating link was going to take some getting used to. It was almost like she'd lived three lives instead of just her own. She had access to everything that Mitchell and Zack had learned over the years. She could see all of their memories, their experiences, their hurts, and their hopes.

Zack answered her question anyway. "Sesturian mating is more accurate," he said as he slid to the side, pulling her with him so that she lay with her head on Mitchell's shoulder and her ass pressed to Zack's groin. "Technically, you're already pregnant. In a few days we'll be able to sense the life growing inside you."

She nodded happily, amazed at how relieved she felt. She'd spent the last few years trying to convince herself that a life without children was what she wanted, but the deep sense of contentment flowing through her proved otherwise. She couldn't wait to have their baby, to bring a small new person into this world. Even knowing that her child had three parents, and an extended family spanning two galaxies, wasn't enough to dampen her excitement. She was exactly where she wanted to be.

But then a niggling thought flashed through her brain. Her sister Kayla hadn't been the woman to give birth, but her link with her lovers meant she'd been able to breastfeed.

Suddenly Mitchell's deep, rumbling laugh filled the room and she could feel Zack's absolute horror. She grinned mischievously as she realized the truth, but couldn't help laughing at Zack's reaction.

"No, beautiful," Mitchell said when he finally recovered a little from laughing. "I don't think Zack has the right equipment."

Zack growled, flipped her onto her back, and pressed her into the mattress with his weight. "No, baby," he whispered as he thrust his hard cock back into her pussy. "The only one who'll be breastfeeding our baby is you."

"You sure?" she asked, smiling as he thrust harder, much harder. "I hear it can be a good bonding experience."

Mitchell laughed and pressed a kiss to her lips. "I love you," he said seriously, "and I look forward to watching you tease Zack for the rest of our lives."

"Tease me enough, baby, and you're liable to get spanked," Zack said, punctuating his promise with a slap against her thigh. She smiled at both of her lovers as the sting morphed into heat, raising her desire higher once more.

Life couldn't get any better than this.

THE END

http://www.rachelclark.webs.com/

ABOUT THE AUTHOR

Rachel Clark loves a great romance.

She happily lives a *romantic* story all of her own with her *wonderful* hubby and *precious* teenagers and menagerie of *perfectly behaved* animals…and, well okay, for the real story you'll need to replace romantic with *hectic*, add *mostly* before wonderful and you can probably guess about the teenagers and animals.

But hey, Rachel loves to read romance and when her life lets her, she scribbles a few of her own.

Also by Rachel Clark

Ménage and More: *Taydelaan*
Ménage and More: *No Use by Date for Love*
Ménage and More: *Accidental Love for Three*
Ménage and More: *A Future for Three*
Siren Classic: *Sarah's Pirate*
Ménage Amour: Sequel to *Sarah's Pirate: Tee-ani's Pirates*
Ménage Amour: Sequel to *Tee-ani's Pirates*: *G'baena's Pirates*
Siren LoveXtreme: *Edwina and the Seven Snowed-in Scientists*

Available at
BOOKSTRAND.COM

Siren Publishing, Inc.
www.SirenPublishing.com